D0806536

About the Author

R. T. Truehall Lives in Adelaide, Australia with her Fiancée, two dogs and two cats. She studied creative writing at Flinders University, and has had a passion for fiction and memoir since childhood. She now works as a Peer Support Worker in the mental health industry, and writes every day in her spare time.

For everyone who told me I could when I thought I could not, and for Mercedes—my one true love—your support lifted me higher than I could have flown had I the wings of an albatross.

R.T. Truehall

NOT DEAD

A CIP catalogue record for this title is available from the British Library.

ISBN 9781786124616 (Paperback)
ISBN 9781786124623 (Hardback)
ISBN 9781786124616 (E-Book)

www.austinmacauley.com

First Published (2016)
Austin Macauley Publishers Ltd.
25 Canada Square
Canary Wharf
London
E14 5LQ

Chapter One

This is not an ordinary vampire story. I imagine you, dear reader to be the kind of person who likes vampire stories, or you would not be reading this very passage. If you are instead groaning inside and about to put my book down because you *hate* vampire stories, then wait! Give it a chance, because I promise you, it's not like the other tales. It's not romanticised, not steeped in history and legend, not televised and not easy to stomach. There is nowhere that you can visit where the movie was filmed, no bar selling t shirts from the television series, it's just the truth. Give it a chance, for at least another page.

Now, I mean it when I say it is not easy on the stomach. This story is *my story,* it's about me and I am—well I was—a complete asshole and I'll warn you now, you're gunna hate me. More than once. Hell, maybe by the last page you'll still hate me but hopefully at least you'll have been entertained. Now that I've talked it up so much, let's begin.

I was twenty-seven when I became a vampire. I can say this with certainty, because on my twenty-sixth birthday I panicked about getting old and counted through all my birthday parties to see if I got the math wrong. I was hoping I was really only twenty-five. I *was* wrong. I had already turned twenty-six a year before. To ease the pain of losing a year somewhere, I decided to go out and get shitfaced.

I called up a few friends to accompany me into oblivion that night. I use the term 'friends' loosely. Back then, when I was still a regular human, I was a completely self-absorbed fuckwit, and like drops of oil in a glass of water, we found each other. There were four of us that hung out, mainly. Tony was my oldest friend. We met in primary school. He showed me his dick and how it was fucked up so he pissed on an angle; he had to stand side-on to the toilet. I remember asking him how come he didn't have it fixed. He replied 'I'm not letting a doctor cut my fucking *dick*'. I was only 12 and didn't have any friends who said fuck. He eyed me for my reaction. I nodded, shrugged and said 'good fucking point' and since then we were pretty tight. He knew what a prick I was, and accepted me for it. I figured that made him my best friend. He was better than me; we both knew it. Relax, I'm not trying to pull on your heart strings, in fact I give you my word that I won't do that once in this whole story. I'm just stating a fact. He wasn't such a bad guy. When we were together he played along, but he had things like a missus and a dog, and he treated them good. I had a dead plant and a goldfish in half a stinky bowl of water. The key to our friendship was he never made me feel bad, but he was honest. I'd never met his other half because he told me straight out 'you're a cunt and I love you. But I am not letting you anywhere near her'. I couldn't blame him, and I told him so. I wouldn't want to introduce me, either. He didn't want her thinking birds of a feather flock together. He also probably didn't want me getting smashed and telling her that we once fucked a prostitute at the same time simply to high-five whilst in the act.

Manny was the friend to make us look good, and trust me, if anyone can make *me* look good, then they are a shocking human being. Manny was actually reasonably good-looking. Tall and naturally well-built, he had one of those bodies that could very easily be whipped into shape with a bit of protein powder and a personal trainer. He was old-fashioned handsome, like a good old boy in the fifties who impressed Fathers with charm and manners, then fucked their daughters and never called on them again. The problem with Manny was that somewhere he got scrambled in the brain and figured that he was only fit to date (read *fuck*) models. If he was mute, that may have worked for a bit. But, he was so rude, entitled and picky, that he rarely got past the one-hour mark in a club before he was soiled by someone's drink. On occasion, he picked up, but owing to his vile nature, the women he brought home were not the type to call him again, so although his conquests were few and far between, they suited his needs. Sadly for so many hopefuls, Manny had a resting nice face, so women often approached him. I have never before or since witnessed a man so arrogant; he would scoff in their face, laugh, turn his back or make some remark like 'ha! I *doubt* it!' It was cringe-worthy, even for me, but he made me look good, so, meh. I often wondered why he hung out with such a motley crew instead of insinuating himself into a more vapid but beautiful social group, and I could never come up with an answer.

Vicki was our token female in the group. I say that like we made a conscious effort to recruit her; we didn't. Once, she got drunk and let Tony and I tag team her, and ever since then we've kept her around in the hope that it will happen again. Go ahead and hate me; I told you I was an asshole. We regularly fucked (Vicki and I, not Tony and me), and I think she would've liked to have been my girlfriend. I didn't love her. I don't love anything, actually, and I didn't want a girlfriend. She wasn't even that great in the sack, I was just incredibly lazy and she didn't make me work hard for it.

So, there we all were, at our favourite bar. It doesn't have a name; it just says 'Bar' over the door in red neon lights. Sometimes the r drops out, so it's just 'Ba' and some corny fuckwit makes a joke about us all being sheep. The place had no highlighting features whatsoever. There would be no reason that this would be anything to anyone except their local for when they didn't want to have to travel further than walking distance. I think it was for that reason alone that it had quite a large and faithful clientele. No cheesy gimmicks, no hispter wank to pull in the brown-shoe-with-ankle-freezers crowd, no drink specials *ever,* just an old jukebox cranked up loud, plenty of darkish corners and bar staff that wanted to serve your drinks and nothing more. The night of my twenty-seventh birthday, the night I was mourning a lost year the sign said 'Bar', bright red and buzzing softly as we shuffled under it. If I had known what was going to happen, I wouldn't have been such a jerk to them. We were a discrepant bunch, but they were the only mates I had.

The jukebox was between songs when we arrived, which I hated. It's like there was an uncomfortable silence followed by the song that would set the mood for the evening. It was, categorically, never a good song. I should have walked out then. There were any number of places we could have gone, and they would have followed me because it was my birthday. But, call me a sucker for punishment or a hopeless romantic cos I thought this time might be different and I strode right up to the bar, droogs in tow. I intentionally didn't think about what song was coming, so of course I was fixated on it, and almost stopped breathing in anticipation.

The first four notes let me know that I was in for a shitty night. I was instantly enraged, indignant and I whipped around, searching for the dickhead that chose it. Fucking Ob La Di Ob La Da by the Beatles, really? *Really*? How many songs did they release? Two hundred odd? I knew for a fact that this jukebox had seven Beatles albums on there, *and* the blue and red compilations. All of those songs and some uncultured half-wit chose *this*?!? They may as well have played Octopus' Garden. Little-known fact: I am a serious Beatles fan. I once threw a bowl of peanuts into a woman's face for alleging that the best Beatles song was Eleanor Rigby. *Eleanor fucking Rigby?!?* I scanned the crowd. It was just after nine on a Thursday, so the place was only half-full. It didn't take me long to spot her. I don't know if she chose the song, and I immediately forgot what I was searching for. She caught me staring at her and it still took me more than a second to look away. It didn't matter; her face was already etched in my memory. I was stunned by the reaction in my body. An icy shiver poured the length of my spine and I felt sick to my stomach with what I could only describe as dread, though that made no sense. As I stood there, staring at the floor trying to make my body respond to reason, I realised I had a massive erection. I was mortified, which surprised me all over again. I had not been ashamed of a boner since grade eight, yet even as I realised that fact, I was making a beeline for the bathrooms so I could splash cold water on it or at least tuck it away discreetly.

I slammed the door open, which scared the shit out of a man who was about to exit. He reeled a bit, but instead of apologising, I shoved past him, grunted and flew into a stall, bolting myself in. I leaned against the door, closed my eyes and tried to calm my breathing. It was hard, since the very fact that I was in a panic and it hadn't happened before was making me feel panicked on top of my panic. I decided to concentrate on my hard-on in the hope that the distraction of making it disappear would end the panic too. I started to think of things that grossed me out, and got as far as dead kittens before it started to subside. The relief was immense; I didn't want to get to picturing my Mum naked. The retreat was swift; it required only a brief jiggle to reposition and I was back to normal. My breathing had slowed, so I opened the door a crack. Nobody was there. I slipped out and stood at the sink, staring at my reflection. 'What the fuck *was* that?' My reflection didn't answer in words, but spoke volumes nonetheless. I looked like shit. I knew I didn't look like that before I left the house, because I was hoping to get laid, even if only by Vicki. My eyes were bloodshot (how?!?) and my cheeks were flushed. My damp hair stuck to my forehead and I had that white shit in the corners of my mouth. 'Ugh.' I wiped it away maybe a little too quickly, because my ring caught on my lip and cut it. 'For *fuck's sake*!' I turned on the tap to splash my face, but not before a drop fell on my shirt sleeve. I didn't give a shit, I just wanted a drink. I wet my face and hair and went back into the bar to find out exactly where Desmond has a barrow, and what Molly does.

Tony was the first to catch my eye. He mouthed 'you ok?' I nodded, took a deep breath, pushed it out and shook it off. I was ready to forget what happened. I was ready to pretend it didn't happen, but no amount of bravado could make me look back over there. I tried to reach my friends using a swagger, but I think it came out more of a scurry. I positioned myself with my back to the rest of the bar, with Tony staring at me all furrowed brow and crooked mouth. Manny was scanning the bar, purveying his land, 'inspecting the produce' as he put it, so he didn't notice a single thing. Perks of having a completely narcissistic mate I guess. Vicki was ordering the drinks and trying to raise conversation from the bartender, to no avail. She glanced over her shoulder and I knew she was looking to see if I was looking and jealous. I just looked away. I should have felt bad; I know I should. But, I didn't. Vic deserved better than me, and I told her on a regular basis. She always insisted that there was good in me, that she could see it, usually right before I told her that I was trying to sleep so could she please stop talking. Undaunted, she plonked a drink in front of me and kissed me on the cheek. 'Happy birthday, asshole' she whispered, and slid her hand lightning-quick over my crotch. I flinched and she pulled back and looked at me quizzically for a moment til I winked and pinched her boob. It was sloppy, but a good save. I was definitely freaked out, but trying to salvage the night.

Manny spun back around and hissed inwards through clenched teeth. 'Did you fucking *see* that chick over there? Who the fuck *is* she?' I didn't move my eyes from my drink. I didn't have to. I knew who he was talking about and I was not about to make the mistake of looking at her again, ever. Plus, it would make Vicki uncomfortable and I convinced myself that I cared and that was why I wouldn't look. It was no shock that Manny was fixated—she was beyond beautiful—though I was surprised; she was curvier than he usually liked. I closed my eyes and saw her. Her hair was perfect black and fell past her shoulders, straight and slick. It reflected the red bulbs on that side of the room, as if it were stealing the luminescence. Her boobs were huge and her cleavage was definitely on show, but it was her gaze that held mine, for once. In that tiny moment, I could see that she was generously built, but she could not possibly have been more alluring. He legs were crossed; her foot had bobbed slightly as she drew me in and I knew she was the cockiest woman I'd ever come across. She wore impossibly high heels, jet back to match her hair and a tight black dress that, despite its simplicity was the single sexiest thing I'd ever seen. She was so white, so, so white that she looked explosive against the black and I knew in an instant that her skin would be smoother than a thousand smooth things. Bizarre, how I was able to recall so much of her when I only looked at her for two seconds, maybe three at a stretch and most of that was into her eyes. They were big and lazily hooded, like it was no effort whatsoever to stare me to death if need be. She didn't blink. From where I was and the amount of time I looked, it would have been impossible for me to determine her eye colour, but something in me knew they were black, or as close as possible to it. But it wasn't her eyes that made me sweat, run and hide. For that last fraction of a second, as I gaped open-mouthed at her, she smiled. It was barely noticeable, and only one corner of her mouth moved, but it was undeniably a smirk. That smile said 'got you' and lasted for such a short time that I could be forgiven for imagining it, but I know I didn't. I shivered, opened my eyes and took a generous swig of my drink. Manny called the bartender over to see what she was drinking. Tony nudged me with his foot, winked and said 'reckon he's got a chance?' I knew that Tony knew I wasn't ok. I also knew that he knew I knew that, so I appreciated his effort. I took the bait, let all my teeth loose into my best birthday grin and laughed 'no fucking way, she is soooooooo outta his league but let him go anyway, I like when he gets shot down.' Tony guffawed appropriately and I thought things might be ok, after all. 'Imma put something better on,' I offered, skulled my drink and headed to the jukebox as Manny drummed his fingers on the bar, waiting for her drink.

From the Wurlitzer, I had a side view of her, sitting alone in a booth. I dared to look in between scrolling, cos I figured that if she turned towards me I had the time to look away. I was legitimately looking for a song: Happiness is a Warm Gun by the Beatles; a perfect in-your-face to whoever put on that rubbish before. As I was scrolling for it, it began to play. Without thought, open mouthed, my head whipped around to her, expecting her to be looking at me, telling me silently that she had read my mind and put it on to fuck with me. She was watching Manny slowly approach and I felt like an idiot. I hunched over the jukebox in a feeble effort to protect myself against I don't even know what, and I covertly peered out from under my armpit. It stank. The fuzzy riff against the steady beat provided the perfect eerie soundtrack for what happened next. He arrived in front of her, and adopted his cocky, legs-apart, I-know-you-wanna-fuck-me stance as he gave her the eyes and the grin and probably the slight crotch thrust. His mouth moved, some sleazy line that actually works on a rare occasion. Suddenly, his face fell slack. He raised his arm, and poured the drink *that he was holding* directly on top of his head. 'Mother Superior jumped the gun' played over and over as the Bloody Mary soaked his hair, flowed down his cheeks, pooled in his ears, and painted his collar. He set the glass on her table, absently turned, and awkwardly made his way through the tables and patrons, bumping into almost every one, as if asleep. He reached the open door, and without pause disappeared through it. His arms didn't swing, he didn't turn to say goodbye, he was just gone. He was sung out by the harmonising 'bang bang shoot shoot' and exquisitely melodic final notes, and I knew I would never, ever listen to that song again.

Chapter Two

Without obviously (read obviously) averting my eyes from *her*, I shuffled back to the bar, shoving my coins away since I never had to pay for my song; I'm a tightwad like that. Tony and Vicki were paused mid-conversation, drinks in hand staring after Manny. Vicki's mouth hung open, and her grey front tooth was on show; she hated that. They looked at each other, then both turned to me. Eyebrow cocked, Tony said 'did he... pour his *own* drink on *himself?* Did I see that right?'

Vicki barked a sharp 'HA! That'll teach that cocky fuckwit! I *love* when he crashes and burns!'

'Vic, you're missing the point. Why would he dump a drink on his own head? A drink he bought for *her-*' Tony leaned around me to look, and I side-stepped.

'Don't look there, man.' He swapped sides, I blocked him. 'I'm serious Tony, please. Don't look at her.' I looked right at his eyes, and he knew I meant it. He could see I was freaked out.

'Dude, what's up?'

'Nothing. I don't know. Ugh. Just don't look at her, I'll tell you later.'

Vicki huffed. 'Oh what, when I'm not around? Fuck you two. I wanna know.'

'It's nothing to do with you, Vic. I just... here and now is not the place or time.'

'It's never the time, cos all we ever do is fuck!'

'Jesus Vicki, take it easy! It's my fucking birthday! I don't wanna talk about it, alright? Can we just talk about something else? Jesus, fuck!'

She sulked but offered 'fine, what do you want to do for your birthday then?'

I glanced sideways at her, then nodded my head towards Tony. 'Threesome?'

'Ugh. Fuck. You.' She slammed her drink on the bar, grabbed her handbag and shoved past us, bee lining for the door.

I shouted after her. 'Aw, c'mon Vic! I was only kidding! Vic! Vic you didn't finish all your drink! C'monnn Vic! Vickiiii... Vic?' And she was gone.

I turned to Tony; his face gave nothing away. I had no idea if he was amused or pissed at me. He looked to the door, back and me and chuckled, 'well that party got small pretty quick. I think you set yourself a record there, champ.'

'Ah fuck em; who needs that drama anyway? Better off you and me anyhow. Drink the place dry. Let's get wasted.' I hailed the bartender.

'I can't stay all night-' he began, and I shot him a look. 'But I can stay for a while! My shout!'

And so it went. I knew what he meant. His missus. He couldn't stay out all night anymore these days, he had to get home to her and their 'fur baby' (retch), but I pretended not to realise that and figured I'd just make him feel too guilty to leave early. It worked for a while; we got pretty sloshed and had heaps of laughs, all the while not looking at the weird broad who made me get a boner and Manny waste a perfectly good Bloody Mary. Looking back, really thinking hard to remember that moment with my friend, my last night as a human, my last (reasonably) innocent good time, I can almost convince myself that I forgot she was there. Almost. Nonetheless, I did a pretty good job of pretending. We were thoroughly drunk (well, at least I was) when Tony looked at his phone.

'Ah shit. It's later than I thought. I'm sorry man, I've gotta go.'

'Oh whaaat? Nooo! It's too early! Stay! Drink! We'll get a hooker!'

For the tiniest moment, the most fleeting of moments, a look of pity flashed across his eyes. It slapped me in the face. 'I can't man, I really can't. I gotta get home...'

'Oh what, to your *missus*? To your *puppy*? I felt my face contort into a mask of mockery and it dripped with petulance. He took a step back and looked me straight in the eye.

'Yeah, actually. To them.'

'Why? They're not the ones who've been there for you all this time...' I thrust my thumb at my chest, 'it's me who has, *me*.'

'Be careful what you say, mate. Let's just finish up a good night, eh?'

'Be careful what *I* say? Why don't you be careful what *you* say?'

'What's that supposed to mean?'

'Well... you've changed that's why!'

'What? That doesn't even make sense!'

'So? Neither do you! You probably wouldn't even fuck a hooker if I got one!'

'No! You're right I wouldn't, because I have a fucking girlfriend!'

'Never stopped you before!'

'Well it's stopping me now!'

'Well... what about Vicki, no more fucking her?'

'What?!? *No more?!?* It happened one time! Years ago! She's not gunna go for that again, you need to let it go!'

'YOU need to let it go!' I thrust a finger in his chest. He threw his hands up, took a few backwards steps and stopped to look at me. There it was again: pity. Not fleeting this time, just there on his face, soft, rotten pity.

'I'll talk to you tomorrow, man.' And he turned and left, just like that. I felt myself swaying.

'What if I don't wanna talk?!? Ever think of that, genius? Your girlfriend think of THAT?' Even I didn't know what I was trying to say anymore. He pushed through the door without looking back.

I slumped back at the bar, reached for my drink, knocked it over and asked for another.

'No.' was the response.

'Yes.'

'*No.*'

'Fuck you.'

'Get out.'

'No.'

'Get the *fuck* out.'

'No. It's my fucking birthday and I want a *fucking* DRINK!'

'Right.' He put down his towel and stormed towards the end of the bar, coming over to rough me up or throw me out, or both. I didn't care. I just stood there watching it all happen.

Then she was between us. I didn't even see her step into my field of vision. It was like I blinked and she was there.

'He's with me, it's ok. You can go back there.' His face went slack just like Manny's, and without a word he turned and practically floated back behind the bar. He took down the bourbon from the top shelf and poured me a double, but I was too petrified to be belligerent about it and I didn't touch it.

She began to turn and I felt myself wince, but I couldn't turn away. Over her shoulder, she spoke, and her voice was silk ribbons on a breeze.

'Get your drink and follow me.'

I did.

I knew I wasn't doing the slack-face-puppet-on-her-string thing, for two reasons: my lips were all of a sudden very dry; I was incessantly licking them, and I had a lot of trouble getting over there. I ricocheted off two tables and realised that I was holding my drink up like a newborn heir, keeping it safe.

We reached her booth. She poured into it and motioned to the seat opposite her. I was frozen to the spot. Slowly, she tapped the table where I was to sit, two hard, deliberate taps that snapped me awake, and I sat so quick I finally sloshed a bit of the bourbon on my hand. I stared at it.

Her voice was impossibly soft, but completely audible over the music. I'd heard of people having a 'musical' voice before, and thought it was a load of shit. What, were these people just getting around *singing shit* like they were on Broadway, permanently? Anyway, I suddenly got it. Her voice didn't sound like music, but something about it made me *think* of music. Don't get me wrong, it wasn't strictly beautiful, just alluring, or powerful, or *something*. It's like I was being mesmerised by a box jellyfish right before being drawn in to excruciating, poisonous death.

'Why are you here?' Even her questions were deceptively complex.

'What do you mean?'

'I mean exactly what I said. Why are you here? And, look at me.'

Every bone in my body felt glued in the posture I'd adopted: looking for the answers to all the world's problems in my glass.

'I said, *look* at me.'

'I don't wanna.' Somehow I all of a sudden felt very sober.

'Why?'

'I'm scared.' And now ashamed.

'I could just make you look at me. I'm giving you a chance to do it on your own, but I *will* make you if you don't.'

I took a breath, as deep as my pounding heart would allow. 'Fuck it.' And I looked at her.

'There you go,' she purred. She smiled, and there was a world in that predatory gesture. In less than a second, I knew I was fucked. She *was* the box jellyfish. My throat thickened, and my eyes got wet. Somehow I was sad for my pathetic, shitty life. 'Now, why are you here?'

God, her teeth were *so* white. 'Uh, it's my birthday. I was getting drunk.'

'Not here at this bar, you imbecile. Here. On this earth. Why do you exist, what is your purpose?'

I stared at her pouty bottom lip. Once, I would have wanted to kiss her. 'Do you mean what do I do... like for a job?'

She closed her eyes and sighed. 'What do you want to *do* with your life? What do you want to be remembered for?'

As every second passed that I didn't answer, my heart sped up. I looked quickly about, like the answer would be floating around my head. I finally managed 'uh... I... don't... I don't know, really...'

'Good, that's what I thought. Drink your drink; it's the last one you'll have as...' she waved her hand to vaguely indicate my person, 'this.'

I didn't want her to ask any more questions. I had a million of my own, but I was scared, confused and sad, so I did what I did best; I skulled my drink.

'You'll be coming with me.'

'Where?' My voice cracked and I added embarrassment to my growing list of ailments.

'Where I am taking you. Get up.'

'What if I don't?' A sudden rush of bravado, or self-preservation, or stupidity. It was very short-lived. She sighed, and simply took off. *How is such a curvy broad so light on her feet,* I thought, just as someone moved my legs for me. Frantically, my head swivelled, searching for who was behind it. There was, of course, nobody and I realised that I didn't feel hands on me, pushing or pulling me, it was just that my legs were being remote-controlled. I grabbed onto the table and scrambled for something to grip, and then my arms weren't mine. My whole body up to my neck was being driven by her. I sat on top of it all, horrified to be a part of this nightmarish ride. As we passed through the crowd, every single person I

28

turned to was slack. Nobody saw me, it was as if I was never there. I saw my jacket, draped on my stool and felt a rush of loneliness for it, if that even makes sense. I missed my jacket already and it would be without an owner or a home. I registered the tears dripping off my chin. I looked back to my captor and felt an inexplicable rush of lust, followed swiftly by anger. Still, I bobbed around on my robot body and followed her out the door.

Once in the night air, she moved faster and so did I. I knew it would do no good to try yelling or screaming, because I would look ridiculous for an instant, and then go all slack-face anyway. I settled for a concentrated effort to stop crying like a little bitch-baby. I couldn't wipe my eyes, or sweep away the snot slug creeping down to my lips. I tried to lick it away, to no avail. I simply followed and hoped I didn't see anyone I knew.

We reached the entrance to an alleyway. We stopped and I felt a rush of control flood back to my body. I staggered a little. She walked into the inky darkness there.

'I'm not going down there.' I said to pretty much nobody. Her acid laugh tickled me from the black alley and I felt her take control again. It filled my body from the ankles up. This time, she must have slack-faced me, because the next thing I remember I was inside, on a couch with a headache. I groaned.

'You must have a pretty bad headache; I walked you into a pole.'

'By accident?'

'No.'

'...oh.'

'Maybe you'll learn to do what I say.'

'Maybe...' I rubbed my head.

She cocked her head. 'What's your name?'

'What?'

'What are you, deaf? What's your fucking *name*?'

I massaged my temples. 'I'm not telling you.'

'Pardon?'

'I'm not telling you anything until you explain why I'm here. Either that, or kill me and get it over with. I don't know how you do the shit you do, but it sucks, you know.'

She guffawed, a sound I hadn't heard her make thus far. 'I don't know if you got the idea yet, mister, but you are not in control here.'

'I can control my mouth.'

A searing bolt of white-hot pain flashed through my temples, and I threw myself on the floor, unintentionally. Some sort of sound was escaping my lips, but it wasn't a scream. If I had to, I don't think I could make it again, not on purpose anyway. As quick as it set in, it was gone and there I was, sprawled on the floor, gasping and conspicuously wet.

'Yes, you can control your mouth. I can't do that. However, I can do lots more than you've seen, so I'm going to ask you again: What. Is. Your. Name?'

'Ulysses, why am I wet?'

'You soiled yourself. Are you serious?!? Fucking *Ulysses*?!?'

I groaned, shifted myself into a sitting position, knees up, arms on top, defeated. 'Yes. I'm serious. My parents are cruel fuckwits.'

'Ulysses... Ulysses...' She rolled it around like a new candy and got up; I flinched. 'Relax, sissy.' She strolled off, behind the couch. For the first time, I looked around. One room. A bed, a couch, a chair and in the corner, a shower. Down lighting illuminated all these things, leaving pools of murky darkness in between.

'Where am I?'

'My place, and shut up. I'm asking the questions.' She reached under the bed and pulled out a container. She picked something out and threw it at me; pants. 'Put these on, you stink.'

'Which was your fault...' I muttered as I unbuttoned my pants.

'What?' Impossibly, she was above me, having crossed the room in an instant. She snatched the pants away. 'Change of plans. Strip naked. Now.'

I stared up at her.

'Now.'

'Oh man...' I felt like crying, but surprisingly, didn't. I knew I was about to die. I don't know why she needed me naked, but I did know it was useless to argue. I kicked off my soggy jeans and peeled my undies off my damp skin. She was right; the smell of my dehydration pinched my nostrils. I saw my penis and was sad. We'd had some good times, my penis and me, but now he just looked small and soft, like he was already dead.

'Hurry up.'

I looked up at her, miserable until I noticed she was completely naked. She was breathtaking. I'd never had an appreciation for bigger girls before. I was too caught up in seeking women whose waists I could wrap one arm around; it made me feel strong. Also, smaller hands made a dick look larger. I was instantly turned on by her power over me, and instantly pissed off at myself for that. My penis wasn't dead yet after all, and I willed it to go back to sleep, to no avail. She looked down and smirked: not in a friendly way. It was 'got you' again. 'Ugh.' She grabbed the shoulders of my shirt and yanked, pulling me upwards. She shoved me on the couch, ripped the shirt off and climbed on top of me.

I covered my junk in a panic. 'No! I don't wanna fuck!'

'I don't *give* a fuck. Move your hands.'

'Noooo...' whining again. Pathetic.

'Look, *Ulysses* (chuckle), you know I can make you if I want. This is about power. I have all of it and you have none. You know I can kill you and I probably still will. This is your chance for one last fuck before you go. What's going on here,' she indicated my erection, 'has nothing to do with me, that's all you and your fucked up brain. Move your hands. I *want* to fuck you, and I *am* going to.'

I stared at her and tried to get my dick to relax one last time. If she was going to rape me, it would be without my input. She raised an eyebrow, but didn't move. Neither did my penis. Her pale skin was completely unmarked; no tattoos, no moles, freckles, stretchmarks (ew), not even a heat rash under those giant perfect titties. How come they looked like that anyway? I thought big boobs were supposed to be saggy? Not these. They were full, but not fake looking and I most definitely wanted to touch them. Her waist was the perfect shape. I thought that under her clothes she would just be... I dunno... round? Instead she looked like a classic painting of one of those naked ladies half wrapped in a sheet holding a baby and sometimes a lamb. My dick was harder than ever. I pointed to it and asked, 'are you doing that?'

'Nope, not yet and it doesn't look like I need to.' She brushed my hand away, which was kinda nice, considering she could have done it with her mind. She gently took my treacherous dick, aimed it, and slid down onto it, arching her back just a little bit.

I was torn, and confused, since I'd never been torn about sex before. Not even if I was fucking a drunk girl. I mean, I'd never raped anyone but I'd gone to places a better man wouldn't have. I was torn because I hated her but definitely wanted to fuck her for way longer than I knew I was going to last. She was tight and wet, and a little less... warm than most girls. Wondering if her body was as cool, I reached up to touch. She slapped me so hard, so fast I saw stars, and I shook my head, tried to focus.

'You *never* touch me without my permission. Never.' She stopped moving, 'Understand?'

I just stared, my hands held up like she was robbing me. With one hand, she reached slowly down, gripped my neck and began to squeeze. '*Understand*?'

'Yes.' I whispered, and I slid my hands underneath my head. I don't know if she ever figured out that it was my own little *fuck you*; she couldn't have known that I'd always wanted to fuck a chick laying back like that, but she seemed satisfied with the move, and she slowly started to grind again, but she kept her hand around my neck.

I couldn't touch her, so I explored her with my eyes. I tried a couple of times to fuck her harder than she wanted, but I couldn't get a rhythm without grabbing onto her ass, so I just let her lead and enjoyed the ride.

Her whole body moved and I was surprised how beautiful it was. She let go of my throat, pushed off my chest with both hands and started to thrust harder. That squeezed her boobs together and I practically salivated at the thought of touching them, god I *needed* to touch her. Her thighs squeezed me and I thought my dick had never been harder than it was at that second. I knew I was about to come, so I looked away, embarrassed and trying to last longer. She didn't break stride, but reached down and turned my head so I was looking into her eyes. I couldn't have looked away if I wanted to. My breathing sped up and I finally slid into her rhythm. She put her cool hands around my neck and started to squeeze.

'I'm gunna come.'

'I know.' Squeezing harder.

'I'm sorry.'

'I know.' Squeezing, smirking, those hooded eyes drawing me in even as my breath drained. She was really choking me, like actually killing me. I started to panic right as I came, and I have never exploded so hard. She made not one sound, and her breathing didn't even change. She just kept staring into my soul, and I actually thought that I was about to end.

Then, she pushed up off me and strode away. I gasped and gasped, just laying there, withering and still musty from my own piss. I couldn't move. Not because she was making me, but because I couldn't hold down a coherent thought. I didn't know where she'd gone, I didn't know where I was, I didn't know *what* she was and I didn't know if I was still going to die. I didn't really care about any of that though, and, believe it or not, I fell asleep.

Chapter Three

When I woke up, it was almost completely dark. After a moment of confusion, I remembered, and realised I was still naked, smelly, very hungover and starving. I groaned and looked around for her. There was only one light on, directly above the chair in which she sat, cross-legged and staring at me. She said nothing.

'Are you gunna let me go or not?'

'No.'

'Then can I have a shower?'

'Please do. You reek.'

I couldn't even be bothered responding. I wasn't exactly sad, just kinda numb, and on my list of problems, my current aroma was number one. Being an asshole makes you unpopular enough, you add smelly to that list and good luck getting laid, ever.

There was no actual bathroom, no curtain even, so I watched her watch me shower pretty much the entire time. I had no room for shame, and I was filthy, so I made sure to scrub my ass crack real good. I'm a pretty hairy guy, so it's easy to work up a funk, especially on a summer's day. Hairy arms, hairy legs, peach fuzzy hairy butt cheeks, anal goatee, neck beard and chest pelt all kept me warmer in winter though. Bizarrely, my back and shoulders were completely hair-free, so I didn't worry about my chest, and just embraced the 80s look when I was shirtless. My poor tiny nipples got very easily lost in the bushiness, which was always a source of amusement at pool parties. I turned the water off and scanned for a towel. Of course she appeared in front of me the next instant with one. I reeled in fright and performed a slippery dance. I finished crouched over, with my arms outstretched; she laughed at me and threw the towel in my face.

'I put pants on the bed for you.'

'That's all I get, pants?'

'Are you cold?'

'Well, no.'

'Then yes, that's all you get.'

I took my time, even drying in between all my toes. I padded over to the bed and slipped on the jeans she left me. They were actually pretty comfy. 'These belong to a guy you killed?'

'Yes.'

I paused, mid-zip. 'Did you at least wash them after?'

'Yes.'

'Ok.' Finished zipping. 'Um, do you have any food? I'm pretty hungry... or even aspirin?'

'I don't have either, but I'll order them in. Not because I feel like being nice to you, but because I want you to think straight, got it?'

'Ah, more questions. Whatever. If you get pizza and coke I'll tell you anything you wanna know.'

'How do you take it?'

I chuckled at the awkward phrasing and wondered how she could be so out of touch. 'Big, like party size. That way there'll be more for later. Go half and half; I'll have meat lovers and you get whatever you want for your half, but don't expect me to play *swapsies* if you get some vegetarian bullshit or something.'

She had a chuckle of her own. 'Oh, I won't be eating any.'

'Sweet, all the more for me. All meat lovers then, with double anchovies.'

'Gross. And do you ever use manners?'

'Not when I'm being held captive.'

'Touché. Hand me that phone please, captive.'

I tossed it to her on my way to the couch. I didn't mind being shirtless actually, I was kinda warm. I closed my eyes and listened to her order. She was super polite, even when the guy on the other end clearly questioned her double order of anchovies. She finished, and brought the chair over to the couch. It must have been heaps lighter than it looked cos she picked it up from the base without letting loose a single groan, or fart. She got comfortable opposite me, cocked her head and squinted her eyes, as if trying to figure me out by guessing.

'You're not overly good-looking, really, are you?'

'Um, that's rude. I do ok.'

'I'm pretty sure you only fuck that Vicki chick, and she has a butter tooth.'

'Heyyyy, go easy, Vic's ok.'

'Whatever. What I'm getting at is, I don't really know what drew me to you. You're average looking, I mean you dress ok, but your hair needs... actually I don't even *know* what it needs...'

I touched my wet mop.

She continued, 'You're really rude, opinionated and have no life goals that I can ascertain. You have a decently-sized penis, and so far that's all I can find that stands out.'

I touched my decently-sized penis and smiled. She rolled her eyes.

'Well, you're mean and you kidnap people. You also control them which is uncool.'

'Ulysses, have you even thought about how I could be doing that?'

'Well, sort-of...'

'And?'

'And I figured you must be, like, telepathic or something.'

'A telepath can read minds, which I cannot do, not in the strictest sense. I can sometimes get vibes, or ideas, but that's it. I am telekinetic, I can move things with my mind, but it's more than that, because I can control other things' minds too, which is how I got you here.'

'Ok... then I don't know. I guess you're a psychic or something.'

She rolled her eyes again. 'No human person can do the things I do, Ulysses. I can plant ideas in people's heads. Your philandering friend brought me a bloody Mary because he asked the bartender what I was drinking. I don't drink alcohol. I put the idea in the bartender's head. It was an ironic joke.'

'I don't get it.'

'I know. When you went to the jukebox, I heard you think Happiness is a Warm Gun, which, incidentally, is my favourite Beatles song. So, I made it play. To fuck with your head.'

So many things I wanted to say; none came out.

'I made your filthy friend tip the drink on his head, then I walked him out. I put the idea in Vicki's head that you only want her for sex, then you suggested a threesome like a dumb idiot and she left of her own accord. I put an image of Tony's girlfriend in his head every ten minutes so he'd feel guilty and not stay too long. Then, I got you here, though I would have preferred if you came on your own, you petulant baby.'

'There's no need for name-calling.'

'*That's* what you're focusing on? Think, actually *think* about how in the hell I could be doing all that.'

'I *have* thought! I don't know! It's fucking scary and to be honest, I don't wanna think about it!'

'Ask me how old I am.'

'What? Why?'

'Ask me.'

'Uh-uh. No way. I'm not *that* dumb. I know you don't *ever* ask a woman her age.'

'I'm telling you to. Remember what happens when you disobey me.'

'Ugh, fine. How old are you... lady whose name I don't know?'

'I'm eight-hundred and seventy-six. And my name is Ellison.'

'Alison?'

'No, moron. Listen to it. Ellison, with an E. And did you hear me? I'm eight-hundred and seventy six.'

'That's impossible.'

'To live that long as a human? Yes.'

'So... you're not human? You look pretty human to me, I mean you have all the right *parts*...'

'I used to be, that's why I look like one.'

'So, then you're a vampire.'

'Yes.'

'I was kidding.'

'I wasn't.' She held my stare.

'Vampires aren't real.'

'That sex seemed pretty real.'

'That's not what I'm getting at. If you're a vampire, where are your fangs?'

'We don't have them, that's a myth.'

'Oh... then how do you, you know... convert people?'

She looked at the ceiling, touched her mouth, then looked back at me. 'Think of it like this: being a vampire is kind-of like having a disease, but it works in complete reverse.'

'Waddaya mean?'

She got up, and I figured I was in for a speech. I wished the Pizza had already arrived. 'Human beings are like cars. They run ok for a while, but with the passage of time, they start to be less... efficient. They break down. Cell regeneration takes longer, joints start to freeze up and things just fail. Then they die.'

'So you're dead? Undead?'

'Shut up and listen. That is the way it works. Time equals degeneration. Being a vampire switches it, makes that work in reverse.' She paused, looking at me, presumably waiting for my response.

'So, you get... healthier?'

'Sort-of. When you are a vampire, with the passage of time comes increased strength, resilience and much reduced need for the things that humans require to make them run.'

I cocked my head, felt like an idiot and un-cocked it then spoke. 'Are you dead or not?'

She pinched the bridge of her nose. 'Ugh. No, idiot. Of course I'm not dead. Dead things are dead. That's it. Dead things can't live. Zombies are a load of bullshit. I am alive, as any vampire is, I'm just so efficient at it, that I don't exhibit the same signs of life that you do.'

'Like what?'

'Well, probably the best example, and the source of most of the misconception is that by now, my heart only beats once every... oh I dunno... Month or so?'

'Once a *Month*?'

She shrugged. 'Or thereabouts. I haven't taken notice for a couple hundred years.'

'What else?'

She stood behind the chair, leaned on it and thought for a few seconds. 'I don't eat food or need to drink water, in fact it makes me sick if I do.'

'So... you survive on blood?'

'Yes, that part's true. As a human, if you got a belly full of blood, it would make you throw up. Reverse it and you have a vampire.'

'But why blood? That's so gross.'

'Ok, sissy. If we can get past the schoolgirl in you, ponder this: blood is the driving life force of humans, they can't survive without it. It makes perfect sense that our evolved systems require that and nothing else to function.'

'But-' and I was pretty proud of myself for thinking this straight with a hangover, 'if you eat all the humans, then there'll be no more food left and you'll all die.'

'Correct. There are two things to consider there. One, we require quite low amounts, and infrequently. Two, we are aware of that, so we have to be careful not to allow our food source to become endangered. It's about sustainability.'

'How do you do that?'

'Think about deer hunters in America. So many people love to hunt deer that you'd think they'd be extinct by now. But, unlike countries where they hunt things like tigers til they're gone, America has a plan. Firstly, people have licences to hunt, and are only allowed to do so in hunting season. This gives the deer time to breed, and replenish the supply. Secondly, some people will purposely buy land and populate it with a certain amount of deer. Then, they'll leave it alone for a few years before they start to hunt. By the time they start hunting the deer, there are too many, so if they *didn't* hunt, the deer would deplete their *own* food source to the point that they starved to death. Now, no more talking until the pizza gets here. I want you to think about what I just said.'

I didn't even realise that my mouth was open until it became so dry I had to lick my lips. Despite my distinctly average intelligence, my hangover and general confusion from the last 12 hours of my life, I was instantly able to grasp what she was saying. I don't think I could have taken in any more info even if she allowed me to.

I jumped out of my skin when the doorbell rang. It was surprisingly normal for a vampire's doorbell. I guess I was expecting something from the Addams Family.

She flew to the door, pointed to me and hissed, 'stay.' I did.

She was completely charming, which seemed necessary, as the delivery guy was clearly nervous. He dropped my coke on the ground which made me sad; now I'd have to wait to open it, dammit. She purred her way through the transaction and tipped him generously. He was smiling but still rushed off when she was shutting the door. She handed me the pizza and coke. I looked around for a table and for the first time realised there wasn't one.

'Why don't you have a table?'

'Why would I need one?'

'I dunno... guests?'

'Well, I've never had one leave yet.' She raised an eyebrow. 'I have furniture on which I like to have sex or sleep. A table is none of those.'

'Fair enough.' I opened the pizza and my stomach growled.

'Do not get any of that greasy shit on my couch, and be careful opening that coke.'

'Yeah yeah I know, I'm not an *idiot.*'

She smiled for a fraction of a second and then settled in to watch me eat.

The pizza was glorious; so very meaty and fishy.

'That smells foul.'

With a mouth full of food, I stopped chewing and a piece of ham fell in my lap. 'Make up your mind, Ellison-with-an-E, if you want me to have the energy to have these *grand convos* with you, then how about you *don't* try to put me off my food?'

'Good point. Let me clarify: that pizza smells very meaty and fishy.'

I plucked the ham off my leg and popped it in my mouth, closely followed by another bite and told her, 'it's s'posed to.'

I ate in silence, with her watching the whole time. Once I was done, I looked for the fridge, found it and went to put the leftovers inside. I thought she might stop me, but she just sat there with a weird grin on her face. I opened the door, and were it not for my love of pizza I would have dropped the box. There was no other food item in there, yet there was only one shelf free for me. Bags and bags of blood were neatly stacked, divided up into different amounts, labelled with names and dates but, surprisingly, not blood type. I guessed, unlike the movies would have you believe, it didn't matter. I slid the pizza inside, found a spot for my can, closed the door, turned but didn't move. She was still looking at me, though no longer grinning.

'You really are a vampire, aren't you?'

'Yes.'

'I thought you didn't need to drink very often... won't these go bad?' I indicated behind me with my thumb.

'They're not all for me; I'm a distributor.'

'Like a drug dealer?'

'No, like a shopkeeper. It's not illegal; it's my job.' She patted the couch.

I sat, feeling a little better and got comfortable for my interrogation.

'I'm not going to interrogate you.'

'How did you know I was thinking that?'

'I told you. Sometimes I get vibes or ideas from people. It's like... for you when someone is very angry, and they *look* angry, *walk* angry and *talk* angry, they don't have to *tell* you they're angry, you'll just pick it up. It's like that, except with much more heightened powers of perception.'

'Oh. Ok. But I thought you wanted to ask me more questions?'

'No, I just told you I wanted you to think straight. I'm about to tell you some pretty heavy shit.'

'Heavier than you're a fucking *vampire*?!?'

'Much. Are you ready to begin? Are you going to be irritating in any way? I hate being interrupted.'

'Well... my coke is in the fridge; I was waiting for it to settle...'

'It will be ok to open in about ten minutes. I'll pause in ten minutes so you can go get it.'

'Ok. Need me to set a timer?'

'No. I've been around for a long time. I'm pretty good at guessing.'

I patted my pockets for my phone. 'I'm gunna time you, see how good you really are.'

'Not on your phone, you're not.'

'Oh yeah. These aren't my pants.' I scanned the room, and bent over to look under the couch; my head throbbed and I shot back up.

'They're not here, and neither is your phone.'

'Ah what? Where are they? Both of em?'

'Your pants were pissy, they went in the rubbish chute. Your phone I made you destroy in that alley last night.'

'Those would have washed! My undies were Calvins and they aren't cheap, so thanks very much for that. And that was a perfectly good phone! What the actual fuck? This is a nightmare!'

She let out a belly laugh. 'Ha! *This* is the news that makes you think *nightmare*?!?' She shook her head, still laughing. 'Fucking *idiot*.'

'Again, rude. And, I was on level 435 in Candy Crush. But whatever. I'm ready.'

She crossed her legs in her chair, and I thought of fucking her in it. 'Ok. I'm going to tell you some stuff, but not too much stuff, because there is a *lot* of stuff. '

'Alright.'

'Ok, so you know that we exist. I'm not sure if you've put two and two together, but... that means... that I can't let you leave here... human.'

'Are you gunna eat me?'

'Well, firstly, we don't *eat* humans. We ingest, or *drink* your blood. But, to answer your question, no I am not. I'm not permitted to. I'm just going to get to the point. I'm going to make you a vampire, and I'm afraid you can't change that decision. I chose you for this. I understand that this may make you sad, but, to be honest, I don't give a shit.'

'Oh. Hm. Am I allowed to make any preparations?'

'No.'

'What about my family?'

'You don't have one, Ulysses.' She really did know a lot about me, evidently.

'Well, what about my fish?'

'To be honest, it would be better off without you, but the fish will still be there.'

'I have a job, you know.'

'You mean delivering pizza two nights a week?'

'Yes!'

'You can still do that.'

'What about Tony and Vic?'

'Yes, fine. You can still see them.'

'Well if I can still see them and do all that other shit, why did you make me wreck my phone?'

'Because I needed an excuse as to why you don't contact them for a few days, and I don't want there to be any trace of your presence here yet. In case you die.'

I threw up my hands. 'Well I'm confused. Am I gunna be a vamp or not?'

'We don't shorten it to that, it's trashy.'

'Ugh, fine. Am I gunna be a *vampire* or not?'

'Yes, in a few minutes.'

'Oh. That's soon... will it hurt?'

'Not much.'

'Really? Ok then, let's get this over with.' I cocked my head and presented my fuzzy neck. I squeezed my eyes shut tight. After a few seconds, I peeked. She was not amused. One eyebrow was arched and her lips were pursed.

'God, Shut *up*.'

'K.' I slumped on the couch, regretting my stupid move.

'Just for a second, can you please forget the fairy tales?'

'Yeah yeah...'

'Ok. So, remember I told you it was like a disease? It's contracted like so many others: by blood-to-blood contact. But, you don't need to drink my blood. That would probably make you sick, and if it didn't, your stomach acid would greatly lessen the chance of my blood taking root in yours.'

'So, you need to cut me and cut you and moosh them together?'

'Not badly. I will prick your finger and mine, and touch them to each other.'

'That's it?'

'That's it.'

'Do we, like, have sex during... or after, or something?'

'No, thanks Hollywood. We can do it and then watch TV. For me, it's not in the least erotic. It's like hiring new staff.'

'We are gunna have sex again at some point though, right?'

'Yes.'

'Ok, then prick away.'

'Are you sure you're ready?'

'Can't get any readier.'

'Do you have any more questions?'

'Yeah, a lot, but if you're not gunna let me go, and I'm about to become immortal, then who's rushing?'

'Good point.' She reached down beside her and pulled out a little yellow pen. 'Come here.'

I knelt in front of her and offered my right index. 'Are you going to say a few words?'

'No.' She stabbed me with the pen.

'What the hell?!? What *is* that?'

'It's a finger pricker for people with diabetes.' She pricked herself. 'Gimme.'

I squeezed my fingertip until a shiny red bead popped up. I looked at it for a second, and tried to think something poignant, but nothing came. I wanted to remember that moment; I guess I did, cos I'm writing about it, but I wanted it to have deep meaning. Instead I thought three things: one, what if she was some weird nutter who was about to give me nothing more than AIDS, two, when would we have sex again and three, would the rest of my pizza go to waste?

seem amused, so I slunk to the couch and sat, quiet. That's when she began to fill me in. It was pretty cool.

As their in-house vampire legend has it, vampires have been around since caveman times. That's like, three and a half million years ago. Vampires and humans were back then all hominines, all the same, and for some reason, some started to evolve differently. It took about five hundred years for them to realise that they were on different rungs of the food chain. It was all pretty primitive, and vampires nearly became extinct; as the more evolved each individual got, the less they could hunt in daylight, and humans became pretty good at protecting themselves during the night. Vampires took a fair while to become strong. It also took ages for them to realise that they could create more of themselves, by spreading their blood to humans. They brought themselves back from the brink of extinction and started to thrive as they learned ways around their weaknesses, and how to maximise their strengths. This was all in Africa, around Ethiopia. Vampires began to spread throughout the world when they followed their food source on the first migration of Homo Erectus from Africa to Eurasia. Now, Vampires are pretty much everywhere, and the most epic news of all I learned was that *they run shit*. Humans think that they're top dog, but it's not so. Vampires happily let them think that, similar to how we let our cats think they're in control of their own lives but the truth is that humans are all here because vampires want them to be, period. Sure, vampires need humans, and they could just farm them in warehouses, like in that movie with Willem Dafoe. Actually, there are some vampires that want exactly that, but the majority don't. Why, you ask? Well, dear reader, I'll tell you. It's because they like their way of life. If they farmed humans, the cat would be out of the bag, and there would be the chance that something could go wrong, putting their food supply in danger. And, the humans would fight. So, they still farm them, but in a much more sneaky (and terrifying) way. And here is where it gets nuts.

I'll start at the top. There is a united nations of vampires. I'm not kidding. They don't limit themselves to countries, just mostly continents, so there are eight main nations: Australia, Africa, North Asia, South Asia, Europe, Upper North America, Lower North America and South America. Each of the nations are divided accordingly into more manageable chunks, with the appropriate hierarchy. I won't give all the examples, but Australia's like this: it's divided into its main sections almost like it is on some Aboriginal Australian maps. There's North state, Kimberley state, the huge desert state, North West state and South West state, all almost the same as the map. East of North state is Rainforest state, and below that is North East state and Eyre state. There's no Spencer (like on the Aboriginal map); it's combined with Riverine state and is bordered on the east by South East state, which includes Tasmania. That's the end of the geography lesson. Why are the states more like Aboriginal Australia than white Australia? Because that's the way it was first, and—accordingly—the first Australian vampires were Aboriginal. Each of those ten states has their own ladders of management etc, and all ten of the heads of state vote on who represents Australia in the United Nations.

Over the years, Vampire societal structure developed, as they realised that if they just created more vampires, and ate more humans, they would eventually all cease to exist. Each nation had its own way of dealing with things, to a point. Eventually, they all converged into a main set of rules. These rules basically revolve around ensuring their survival as a species, which is basically how it is for humans too, in my opinion. We go to work to earn the money to buy the food to feed ourselves and our kids so our kids grow up nice and strong and can go to work too. Now and then, people break the rules and try to do things their way, but they are punished for it. That happens in the vampire world, too, but I'll get to that.

There are three main types of vampires: government (rule makers and enforcers), who take care of keeping everything hush hush and running smoothly, harvesters, who collect blood to keep the vampire population from going rogue, and vendors, who operate the facilities from where vampires can collect their sustenance. For me, this fact alone raised an important question.

'Why can't vampires just kill people by themselves, like they do in the movies?'

'Because then there would be lots of unnecessary killing and waste of food. Also, we would run a much higher risk of being discovered.'

Ellison explained it by going back to the deer example. So, the harvesters are licensed to harvest. No vampire may kill a human without that licence. The licences vary from state to state, and sometimes even from area to area within a state. A harvester's licence dictates how many people he or she can kill in a given period of time, within the 'hunting season' dates of that area, and get this: the reason they are specific to areas is that it depends on how the food is being *farmed* in that area. No kidding. Farmed. This blew my mind a fair bit.

'We're not animals! You can't *own* us!'

'You're one of us, now.'

'You know what I mean.'

'It's not that we own them, *per se*. Human beings have free will, and we want them to. Yes, a certain number of people will move away from where they were bred. We factor that into population growth. It all comes out in the wash. Bigger human populations equal bigger vampire populations.'

'Well, what if you make too many vampires? How many have you made?'

'Good question. You can have your coke now if you want.'

I relished the acidy sweetness of the coke, and thought she was full of shit about the fact that one day I would no longer consume food or drink. She went on. Every vampire is allowed to make a certain number of new vampires per certain period of time. That period of time depends on the country in which they live. The reason for this is obvious: too many vampires equals not enough food in the long run. Not just that, though, then there would be too many of them for the jobs that need to be done, which means idle hands, which means vampire crime. I asked her why a vampire would particularly want to create other vampires, especially if what she said is true, that you can still be friends with humans. Her reasoning was simple. As time goes by, we live in the night more and more, which means that a lot of the people we hang out with are either drinkers and partiers (which gets old), or we have to let them go anyway, when it becomes obvious that they are ageing and we are not. This means that we often have either shallow friendships, or none at all. Essentially, vampires get lonely.

'Well, what if you create someone and they don't wanna hang around?'

'A new vampire has to stay with its maker for one hundred years. After that, it is a choice and they can move on if they want. Most do, hence the desire to create again.'

'How do you enforce that?'

'The vampires in the government roles. They find the ones that abscond and return them.'

'And if they keep running away?'

'They are punished.'

'I see... so I have to stay with you for *a hundred years*?'

'Yes. Or, you can choose death.'

'Isn't it a crime for a vampire to kill another vampire?'

'Sometimes yes, sometimes no.'

'Isn't it, like, really hard to kill a vampire?'

'Not particularly, especially a new one. You're no stronger than an hour ago. I could snap your spine with my brain.'

'Don't we get better? Like, stronger?'

'Yes, but we're not supernatural. We don't need a wooden stake to the heart to die. I mean, that'll kill us, but that would kill anyone. Even if you have a really old, really strong vampire, you can just cut its head off. Nothing can survive without a head.'

'*Aren't* we supernatural though? I mean, living *forever*? That's not normal.'

'Normal for whom?'

'Well, humans I guess...'

'Physa acuta snails are hermaphrodites and can impregnate themselves. That's not normal.'

'Can vampires *impregnate themselves*?!?'

She actually slapped her forehead. 'No, you're missing the point. The miracle of how life even begins is bizarre. How do we get a soul? How do humans' hearts keep beating? Why do they sometimes just stop? All of this is magic, and none of it is normal. And, thank *god* you can't impregnate yourself.'

'Hey!'

'Well, you're not exactly *Nobel Peace Prize* material.'

'I can't argue with that. So how often are you allowed to make a new vampire?'

'In South West state, once every three hundred years. It used to be every two hundred, but the human population has stagnated.'

'Why, did you guys kill too many?'

'*Us* guys...'

'Whatever...'

'No, it just happens sometimes. Factories close down, people become unemployed and they don't have as many children. The human economy is on its way back up, but they're not out of the woods yet so right now, it's still once every three hundred.'

'So you've been alone for two hundred years?'

'No. My last companion was here until fifty years ago.'

'Why did he leave? He get sick of you being too pushy?'

'He committed a crime and I had to kill him.'

'...Hm. Well that got awkward.'

'You asked.'

'So... then for fifty years you've just bummed around?'

'I don't "bum around"; I have a job. I also have a licence to harvest, if I want to. It's a level three licence. That means I don't *have* to harvest as my job, that's level one.'

'What's level two?'

'That means you're the first to be called up to harvest if things get... dire.'

'And level three?'

'It means I *may* harvest three humans per harvest season, but I need a new permit every season, and I have to sell two thirds of what I harvest. The rest I can keep.'

'For yourself to drink?'

'Sometimes. I'm also permitted to sell it and keep the proceeds for myself, which is how I save money; I don't get paid all that much for being a vendor.'

'I kinda thought all vampires were rich...'

'Another myth. How would we be? We're pretty much the same as humans in that regard. Some of us are wealthy, and we get that way through hard work. Some lead a comfortable existence and are happy that way. Some live below the poverty line, and that becomes a problem.'

'How come?'

'Well, think about it. If they don't have a licence to harvest, then they can't collect their own food; it's illegal. If they don't have the means to be a vendor, then they can't earn money that way, either. If they don't go into government... then they're useless, and they usually turn to crime.'

I finished my coke and let that settle in. 'Crime? Like killing humans without a licence?'

'Mostly. Some just stoop to typical human crimes like theft and fraud. In the rare circumstance, some use the skills they've developed to coerce humans to commit crime or offer their blood voluntarily.'

'Why wouldn't they just take the easy road and get a job?'

'Why don't some humans? Why are human jails full?'

'Ohhh... good point.'

'Some just aren't... very good at being vampires.'

'Don't all of... *us* get stronger over time?'

'Stronger and better as a functioning unit, yes. Better at the skills that make some of us lethal killers and master manipulators... not necessarily.'

'What, so you mean there are vampires out there that aren't particularly stronger or faster than the average human?'

'Yes.'

'What a rip!'

'I have to admit, I agree with you, but that's the key element about vampirism; it's not magic, it's biological, so anything can happen. We don't all of a sudden become these beautiful, swift, strong mythical creatures. It takes time, and practice.'

'So, if I don't practice at shit, then I might turn out a dud?'

'Totally possible. If that were the case, I'd kill you.'

'Oh what? Why?'

'Because you would be an embarrassment to me.'

'Oh. Ok.'

I had a sudden rush of anger. It all hit me at once; the fact that I was now different, changed. It wasn't my choice and there was nothing I could do about it. I was going to live forever, potentially in utter loneliness and poverty. There was a huge chance of both of those things becoming a reality, because I was well aware that I was a complete asshole and was lucky to have the few friends that I did, and also because I was not particularly talented at doing anything physical. I crushed my coke can and threw it on the floor, jumped up and rushed her, screaming 'why'd you pick me, you bitch?!? Why?!?' I'm not going to say I've never hit a woman, because I have. I am an average sized man, neither big in stature nor small, and there are some *tough* chicks out there. If they hit me first, I hit back. I suppose it's true that I've never hit a woman *first*, so this was out of the ordinary for me. Naturally, she saw me coming a mile away, and deflected my attack so that I was flung onto the floor and again, I slid. I think I got a splinter in my chin. I bit my tongue and tasted blood but had no time to think on it, because before I could even begin to flip myself over, she did it for me, and pinned me to the floor.

'I chose you because of this very behaviour. You're uncaring, and very selfishly emotional and angry a lot of the time. I've been watching you for *ten years*.' She slapped me across the face, hard. I tasted more blood and felt tears spring to my eyes. She stared deep into them and I felt she was daring me to cry. I refused. As she held my gaze, she licked my blood from her fingers, slowly. I was instantly hard.

'No! Not again! Not when I'm angry! I fucking hate you! I do NOT give you permission to fuck me!'

She laughed: a flat, evil sound, and I felt that heart-thumping fear from the bar the night before.

'RAPE! RAPE!' I never thought I would hear myself frantically screaming that.

She laughed again, leaned down and whispered in my ear: 'scream all you like. I've had years to make this place sound-proof. I prefer it if you struggle.' She reached down and tore through all the buttons on my fly; they pinged across the floor.

'NO NO NO NO NO!' I summoned all my energy and shoved her in the chest. She did not budge, gasped and bit her lip, pinned my arms down and straddled me. It seems that she had not even been wearing underpants. I gritted my teeth and let out what can only be described as a growl with some yelling and wailing. Frustration brought back the tears and this time they spilled over and over and I didn't even care. I focused all my energy into my penis and tried to make it wither. She grinned wider and began thrusting so hard that my bare back squealed against the floor. Suddenly, it happened. I felt it begin to soften! He was on my side!

She stopped moving, cocked her head and looked me in the eye. 'Naughty naughty...' she murmured, and I felt it in my feet, creeping up my ankles, my shins, my knees, my thighs. That awful nothingness left me in her control and I felt my poor penis harden up. Then my chest, then my arms and I figured she was going to knock me out. She didn't. She left me conscious, just a head attached to a sex toy. I turned my head to the side and silently cried. Surprisingly, she let me.

When she was done, she got up, looked my direction over her shoulder and said 'clean yourself up.'

'Why don't you make me.'

'Because you need to learn that you are mine. MINE. I made you, and *I own you* until you are strong enough to prove otherwise. The sooner you get that in your head, the easier your life will be. The longer you take, the more I do what I want with you. Now get up and *fucking* shower again, *now*.' She turned to look at me, when I didn't move. 'Last chance. If you make me make you, you will regret it.'

I got up. My hips were stiff, my chin hurt and I thought I felt a friction burn on my back. I wiped my face and headed to the shower, avoiding her gaze the whole time. I didn't know what to feel, there was so much going on. I'd just been raped by a vampire. It's not every day you hear that in your head, especially as a dude. I vowed one day I would hate fuck her so hard that she called me *her* boss. I turned on the water and watched it go down the drain. I let my mind go numb.

Once I was done, I went to the fridge and pulled out the pizza. I fell onto the couch in just a towel. She gave me the one eyebrow.

'If you're going to keep fucking me then I may as well stay naked.'

'Fair call. Would you like to know more about your new life?'

'Yes Ma'am.'

'Do I need to remind you to keep the pizza off the couch?'

'No Ma'am.'

'Very well. Where was I?'

Chapter Five

She told me more, lots more. I ate that pizza and eventually ordered another, and another. Days passed—I don't even know how many—but one thing I did know was that I noticed no perceptible change in my strength or physique. I was pretty pissed about that, but Ellison kept telling me to be patient. After maybe a week of pizza and not-really-consensual sex, she told me I could go out. I couldn't really believe it, and wasn't too sure where to go. I decided on my house, to see if my fish was still alive. I asked her how she would know that I wouldn't just run, or tell everyone my new secret. She told me I was welcome to tell people, if I wanted to end up in the nuthouse. I had no way to prove it, and certainly no exceptional skills as evidence. As with the running, she reminded me of the government vampires, and flippantly told me that she had actually been very gentle with me, and that some vampires were gay men. She gave me that direct stare and I completely understood.

I was a bit paranoid about being watched or followed, and to be honest I would have been content to just start living with her right away. She told me that while I was still 'disgustingly human', with 'disgustingly human habits' that I would have to at least spend some time for these first few months in my own place. So, I figured I would still need to pay rent, and for that I needed my job.

She let me out in the daytime, and the sun was so incredibly bright after a week in the dark. I didn't think I was any more sensitive to it than I'd been before, though you wouldn't know it to have seen me. I *looked* like a vampire: squinting, shielding my eyes, scurrying from shade to shade. And, the clothes she'd given me to wear were utterly unacceptable. For pants, I had a pair of those horrible sand coloured cargo slacks that *zipped into fucking shorts at the knees*. To make matters worse, they even had a second pair of zips halfway down the shin! What the *actual* fuck? The shirt she gave me was a polo. A SALMON COLOURED POLO. It even had that little picture of a guy riding a horse on it. I prayed I wouldn't run into anyone I knew as I scuttled for my place.

My fish was, surprisingly, not dead. I didn't want to care for it anymore but—surprisingly again—didn't have the heart to flush it, so I poured it into an old bread bag, tied a knot in the top and set off for the aquarium. In hindsight, I still can't believe I did that, but it was a pretty confusing time for me.

I stumbled in from outside, and almost dropped the fish. I blinked wide, shaking my head in an effort to rid my eyes of all that light and bumped into the counter.

'Can I... help you?' The sales assistant frowned and bent closer to scrutinise the murky water and the one lonely, sad looking goldfish.

'Yeah, I, uh, I wanna return this fish, please.'

'For a *refund?*'

'Oh. No, not for, like, money, I just... can you take it? I can't keep it anymore.' I slid the bag over to her.

'Sure...' she took the bag and walked out from behind the counter. She stopped in front of the first tank. She pulled out little shelf, and placed my grimy fish bread bag on it. Carefully, she opened the lid to the tank, and from the top of it produced a little green net. She untied my knot and while supporting the bag, dipped in the net. The poor dumb guy didn't even fight, he just let her scoop him up. She dipped him in the tank and he didn't move. Then he suddenly zipped off, and into the far corner of the tank, where all the other fish were collected.

'Weird...' I muttered, and she jumped, which made me jump. At some point, I'd followed her and crept so close that I could see my breath on the glass. That was a surprise in itself, never mind that the fish were all crammed into one space.

'Why are they doing that?' I whispered.

'I do not know...' she replied, taking a step sideways, away from me. I wondered if I smelled. I tried to surreptitiously sniff my opposite armpit; there was nothing off that I could detect. She put her little net away, closed the tank and slid the shelf away. 'Let me know if you need anything else...' and she slunk off. I moved to the centre of the tank. The fish moved, as one and collectively hovered in the middle of the back wall. I moved further over and they moved to the other corner.

'What the fuck...' I sprang back to the other side, and they shot off to their original corner; a couple bumped into the glass. I moved to the next tank; same result. I kept strolling and peering into the tanks. Every single fish tried to get as far away as possible from me, there was no denying it. In the last tank, all the fish moved, and all the snails fell from the glass, sucked their feet inside and dropped to the sand, hiding in their shells.

In the middle of the aquarium, there was a huge hexagonal tank on a pedestal. It must have been two metres high. I'd always loved that tank. It always had all the coolest fish in it. There was a lion fish, a stone fish and a pufferfish. I stood in front of one pane, and watched the lion fish cruise around, the first in the store who seemed unaffected by my presence. Out of the corner of my eye, I noticed movement, and looked to the counter. Three staff were watching me and one of them had his mouth open. All of them scrambled to look busy. I looked back to the tank. The Lion fish had crept closer to me, and the stone fish appeared also. They approached slowly. The puffer emerged and immediately took in water; I saw its funny little teeth and thought how happy it looked. It lumbered over, keeping one eye on me, and one on the other two. Gently, I laid my hand on the tank wall. The Lion fish braced and almost doubled in size, the stone fish frantically zipped back and forth, and the puffer whipped its tail rudder into action and head butted the glass, a spiky, crazy-eyed ball. I stumbled backwards and fell into a display of plastic hermit crab tanks. They clattered everywhere and I reeled, trying to catch them, or save them, or something.

Two staff rushed over, though they looked in pain and like they would rather be home in bed.

'I'm sorry... I didn't see them there...' I managed, while they averted their eyes and collected the homes.

's ok,' one of them muttered to the floor.

'No problem,' the other whispered before his voice cracked.

I figured the best thing that I could do was leave, so I ran for the exit without another word. The automatic doors didn't open wide enough in time, and I caught my shoulder as I lurched through. It spun me sideways, and I hit the ground hard enough to let loose a hefty 'ooof'. I even rolled once or twice. I felt all of their eyes on me, and without even a glance backwards, I scrambled onto my feet and fled.

I didn't stop running until I had my back to my front door. My mind was racing. Amid the swirling sea of thoughts, one thing floated to the surface. Those fish were scared of me, except the nasty ones with potent defence mechanisms and few natural predators. Could it be happening this fast? How could they tell from *inside* their tanks that I was a threat? My chest was heaving; I was still hectically sucking in air. I wondered how long until I'd be better at running and stuff. I looked down at my clothes and groaned. I'd forgotten I was wearing that crap. I shed the embarrassment and headed to my own familiar shower, wondering how I was going to explain my week's absence to my boss. Drunken binge? Kidnapped by sexy lingerie models and tied up as a sex slave? Ugh. That last one was too close to home. I decided to tell them that I was in an accident and had been in hospital.

I was enjoying a thorough sudsing when I felt something tickling my feet. I frantically wiped the soap from my face to check it out; I *hate* spiders. I initially thought it was exactly that: a million tiny spiders engulfing my feet and then I realised it was hair. Terrified, I felt my head all over, but everything was fine. Then I saw my chest. I looked like the victim of a hilarious prank involving hair clippers and lots of alcohol. The front of my body looked like I should also rightly have a dick and balls drawn on my face in sharpie. I gingerly rubbed it, and more hair coated my palms. It was like the shower was laced with hair removal cream. On one hand I was scared, on the other I was fascinated. It'd always been way more trouble that it was worth to try to remove all my fur for beauty's sake, but I was guessing this was it going for good. I rubbed around until it wasn't coming out anymore, on my chest and arms. I wondered if I'd never grow a beard again. I finished up and checked myself out in the mirror. I had a reflection: another myth busted. I was much less hairy, though there were still patches left. I took some time to study my naked body. I wished I'd thought to do it a week ago. Even so, I was *sure* that I was looking better, *and* I'd eaten nothing but pizza for a week, literally. I still didn't have any definition really, but my pudgy teddy-bear belly was definitely smaller, and my little man titties were too. Those were pretty much the only things I could notice, but combined with the reduction in hair, it made for an overall positive picture.

I realised I needed to take a shit. I was irritated; it always seemed like a waste of a shower to do one after. I farted on the way and quickened my pace. I wondered if it would be easier to wipe since I had less hair down there. I needn't have worried; it was a one-wiper. I looked in the bowl and saw the tiniest poo I'd ever done. 'Is that *all*?' I asked it. I didn't feel like I still had any more to come, so I got dressed in undies and some loose shorts that seemed to hang extra low. I headed to the fridge, opened the door and slammed it shut. Something was wrong. There was definitely something dead in there. I opened the sink under the cupboard to grab the bin and was punished again, but there was no avoiding it, so I grabbed it out and held my breath while I tied the bag and dumped it outside the front door. I figured I must have had some meat in there for it to smell that bad. I grabbed a new bag and stood in front of the fridge, gathering myself. I flung open the door and just started sweeping everything off shelves into the bag. Every single thing had to go, regardless of what was rotten and what wasn't. I gagged twice. With that bag out front too, I took the spray n wipe and grabbed the sponge. On a whim, I smelled it, gagged again and went to get a new one from the bottom drawer. There weren't any, so I grabbed an old pair of undies and used them instead. I scrubbed the fridge from top to bottom. Once the rotting smell was gone, and I could think straight, I realised I was hungry. The cupboards offered a shitty menu: rice, a tin of corn and a tin of baked beans. I chose beans. I opened the microwave and it reeked. In a rage, I grabbed it, ripped it out of the wall socket and threw it outside the door too. I heard it smash as I slammed the door.

As I sat on my cracked 'leather' couch eating my cold beans from the can, I heard a phone receive a text message. It obviously wasn't mine, but it did seem to come from the shitty cargo zip-offs and salmon polo pile. I ate the last few beans slowly, casually watching the rumpled bunch of middle-aged Dad clothes. It beeped again. I had obviously not noticed the weight in the pocket, because when I lifted the pants I'd been wearing all morning, a phone fell out, and beeped once more, as if to say 'bout time!'. It looked new. It was a smart phone, a Samsung. The lock screen picture was me, sleeping naked, my tired, sad penis laying soft against my thigh like he was snoozing too. 'What the...' I asked nobody as I slid my thumb across the screen to unlock it. The home screen picture was utterly terrifying. It was me again, in slack-face mode. Again I was naked (what's with that). I was standing, arms outstretched like a zombie Christ. I was looking into the camera, but 'I' clearly wasn't present. That look haunted me for years from that day. It was complete vacancy, just a deep, bottomless nothing. The more I looked at it, the more it didn't even look like me, because I had no memory of posing for the picture. Ellison was crouched in front of me, unsmiling. In one hand, she held my penis, flaccid but stretched to a length I wouldn't have thought possible. I touched my actual penis to make sure it was ok. In her other hand: a knife, held to the base of my dick. I thought of Tony, and cutting dicks in general. 'You're so *fucking* sick' I whispered, and hated myself for feeling a rush of lust at the fact she was naked too. I had three new messages. They read:

'Kept your sim. Enjoy your new phone.'

'Obviously, change either picture and I WILL punish you.'

'Let me know when you get this.'

The pictures were clearly reminders. I hated her so much. I liked the phone though.

I checked the other messages. There were several that had been read, but not by me. First cab off the rank: two from work. I did some math. I went missing on a Thursday. I usually delivered pizza on a Monday through Wednesday. So, I'd missed three shifts, and my new phone told me that it was a Sunday, so if I sucked up, I might be able to work tomorrow night. My bosses were cool. The texts weren't even mad, just worried. I text back: 'had an accident out of town. Phone dead til I got back today, sorry. Can I still work tomorrow?' Then, Vic:

'ur an asshole'

'I cnt blv u said that' Oh yeah, I'd suggested a threesome.

'u could at least answer'

'I'm sry i yelled at u'

'fuck uly what do u want me 2 say'

'i miss u'

'uly r u ok'

'hello?'

'I'm worrid'

'pls cal me'

That last one was two days ago, I could work with that. The only other messages were from Tony:

'I'm sorry things got out of hand, dude. I didn't mean to be an asshole, but you were a dick too. Friends?' That was three days after my 'party'. Then, just one more, another three days later:

'Come on man don't be mad. I said I'm sorry...' Four days since that one. I wasn't concerned. Tone and I had been mates long enough that I could salvage that. Nothing from Manny but that wasn't unusual.

For the first time in over a week, I actually felt ok. I probably still had friends, I probably still had a job, I didn't have to look after that fish anymore and I wasn't, like, bursting into flames in the sunlight. Apart from losing some hair, I wasn't really being affected by this vampire thing. The more I thought about it, the more I wondered if it even happened at all. Maybe Ellison just drugged me. Maybe I'd just been on acid the past week. Maybe she wasn't actually controlling my body, and it was all part of the trip. Maybe.

There was a knock at the door and I jumped so hard I knocked my can off the couch and it rolled underneath. I peeked through the eye hole: speak of the devil, it was Manny. I let him in. He stood in the doorway, frowning at me.

'What the fuck?'

'Hello to you too. Do ya wanna come inside, or just stand there staring like you've gone super gay for me?'

He pushed past me and headed straight for the couch. He flopped down and flipped his hand towards the door. 'What's with all the rubbish?'

'Uh, it was all gone bad, I've been away a few days...'

'Have ya?' That's all the probing he did. Manny was mostly interested in talking about Manny. 'Got anything to eat?'

'No, and I'm starving. I just ate a can of cold beans.' I scratched my belly, ended up with a clump of hair and shoved it in my pocket before he noticed.

'Wanna get a pizza? My shout.' That was the weird thing about Manny. He was a gigantic narcissistic jerk, but flush with money and not shy of throwing it around.

I shuddered, but I *was* flat broke. 'Sure, that'd be ace.'

'Meat lovers?'

'Uh, actually I might get Hawaiian...'

He leaned back and looked at me again, this time squinting. 'Are you sure *you've* not gone gay? Shaving your chest? *Hawaiian?!?*' I looked at my chest. I don't know how he could possibly think it was shaved; a pre-pubescent teen could've done a better job. I wasn't about to correct him though.

'Nah, just want something different...' and I headed to my closet for a shirt. 'Want me to order?' I threw over my shoulder.

We sat in my shitty apartment eating half-decent pizza (there was something wrong with the ham on mine and I picked it all off) and watched the telly. Almost two hours passed before he broached the subject.

'Can I ask ya something?' He looked at his hands.

'I'm not gay and I won't be your boyfriend.'

He didn't laugh. 'I'm serious. It's about your birthday.'

I had one trick up my sleeve to try to end that conversation: 'ah don't worry about leaving early man, it's fine, all water under the bridge.' I sat frozen, willing him to take the bait.

'See, that's just it. I don't *remember* leaving.'

Grasping at straws: 'Well, you were pretty wasted...'

'Yeah but when I woke up in the morning, I'd only spent ten bucks, and the only drink I remember buying was that Bloody Mary for that chick. I *know* I didn't buy any drinks before that.' He looked at me then, into my eyes, and he was scared. 'Uly, I'm actually pretty freaked out about this. It's never happened before... I think I'm going crazy... the next morning I was covered in tomato juice, like it was in my *ears* and shit...' I just looked at him, I had no idea where to go from there. 'Can you, like, fill me in on anything? It's driving me nuts.'

I sat there and knew this was to be the first of many lies. I looked at my lap, pretending I was trying to figure out how to tell him something awkward. I started to speak while still looking down, and had a fleeting thought that I was a pretty good liar, actually.

'Well, I wasn't gunna bring it up... I thought maybe you'd taken something...'

'What, like drugs?'

'I dunno, I guess?'

'Why, what happened?'

'Well, you took your drink over to... that chick, and started talking to her. She asked you to sit down and you gave her the drink. We were all watching cos we made bets on what would happen.'

'Waddaya mean, bets?'

'Well, like Vic bet you'd crash and burn, and Tony and I bet her you'd hook up.'

He smiled for a moment. 'Atta boy...'

'Anyhow, it looked like it was going ok, and then all of a sudden she threw the drink at you, like all over your face.'

'What a bitch.'

'I know, right? Vic thought it was great and hassled us to collect her winnings straight away. We didn't notice you walk back over, just, kind of all of a sudden you were there...'

'Well, what did I say?'

'You were kinda spaced out. You told us you had to go home and before we could even say anything, you were out the door. It was pretty weird... like I said, all we could figure is that you took something and maybe it was too intense. Vic thought you were being a baby cos you crashed and burned.'

79

'Maybe she drugged me.'

'Maybe, but I didn't see you drink anything, you only had the drink you bought for her... maybe you had... an episode...'

'What the fuck does *that* mean?'

'Well, maybe you had, like, a mental break or something, I dunno...'

'A *mental break*?!?' He was starting to look kinda mad.

'Look man, I dunno, don't get all worked up about it, it wasn't like you made a big scene or anything.'

He slumped back in his seat. 'You know... I don't even remember what she looked like...'

'She looked like a fucking bitch.'

'Yeah...' He picked up the remote and started to look for something better to watch.

Chapter Six

After Manny left, I crashed. My own bed had never felt so good, though the sheets stank and I'd had to change them. The next morning, I had only one text awaiting me, from Ellison:

'I told you to let me know when you found the phone. Do not make me come and get you.'

I replied, 'sorry. Got the phone. Was sleeping.'

She didn't text back; I didn't care. I was feeling pretty good, like, rested or something and I suddenly had the idea to check myself out. I was disappointed that I looked the same, though I'd lost more hair, and the rest came off in the shower with a bit of scrubbing. I liked the new smooth me, and the lack of pubic hair made my dick look bigger. I decided to pay Vicki a visit.

She peeked through the curtain beside her front door, and threw it open when she saw it was me.

'You fucking jerk! A week? Over a week actually, and no response?'

'I'm sorry Vic, my phone broke.'

'And this is the first time you thought to come by and let me know you're ok?'

'I was out of town... I got in an accident...'

'What? Out of town where? Are you ok?'

'Just... it doesn't matter, I'm fine now, can you let me in?'

'Ugh.' She stepped aside and waved grandly. Her house smelled like pea and ham soup, the way I remember my Mum making it when I was a kid, from pigs' trotters.

'Are you cooking...soup?'

She frowned at me. 'What?'

'Nothing... just kinda smells like pea and ham soup... in here...'

'Yeah, like two weeks ago. How the hell can you still smell that?!'

I ignored the question, wishing I'd never brought it up. 'I'm glad you're home, Vic. I was missing ya.' It wasn't a lie, I actually did enjoy hanging out with her sometimes; it was stress-free and occasionally fun. Plus, the sex. I wondered how long until we could get to that. I decided not to push it, and I headed for the couch. 'Wanna watch some telly?'

'Wanna fuck?'

'What?' I turned and looked at her. She smiled— mouth closed on account of the butter tooth—and unbuttoned her tiny shorts. They fell to the floor, followed by her underwear. I was literally already making panties drop, and she hadn't even seen my hairless chest yet. She circled the couch, knelt in front of me and unzipped my fly. It occurred to me that I should feel guilty: guilty for fucking Ellison when I knew Vicki wouldn't want me to (not that I could help it), guilty for fucking Vicki when I knew Ellison probably wouldn't want me to and guilty that I knew already that while fucking Vicki, I was going to pretend she was Ellison and that I was finally the one on top. But I didn't feel guilty, in fact I'd always wanted to have several women on the go, and it was actually happening. Guilty could get fucked. I let Vicki go down on me for a while, then I pushed her on the floor and pushed inside her without returning the favour. I didn't kiss her, I didn't make any of the usual effort I did to keep her on the line, like telling her that she was hot, so tight, so good, etc. I just pictured Ellison and fucked her hard. I flipped her over and pulled her to her knees. I pushed inside her again, grabbed her hips and pounded. She thrust back at me and squealed. I grabbed a fistful of her hair and pulled, I didn't care if she came, but I did, and it was the best I'd ever remembered.

I flopped down beside her on the rug. She was panting, I wasn't.

'What was that?!' She breathed.

'Waddaya mean?'

She propped on an elbow. 'You're usually so... lazy.'

I took it as a compliment. 'Well, I told you I missed ya. Got anything to eat?'

83

'Ugh. Typical.' She got up, put the shorts back on without the underwear and I made a mental note to fuck her again before I left. She called out from the kitchen.

'Ham sandwich?'

My stomach turned. 'Uh... no thanks. maybe just... tomato and cheese?'

'Whatever...' it almost sounded sing-song. She was in a good mood. For a weird moment I felt close to her, and wanted to tell her my secret. Thankfully it passed. She appeared with my sandwich and a can of coke. She knew me better than I'd ever cared to know her. I was starving, and expecting my snack to taste great, which it did, but the coke seemed sugarless. I chugged it anyway. She apologised for running out on my birthday, I apologised that she felt I only used her for sex, though I wasn't in the least sorry.

We watched TV and it felt comforting, familiar. Vicki kept her house real clean, but I suspected that had more to do with methamphetamine use than a desire for cleanliness (being close to godliness). Even though the place was as spotless as usual, I could smell sex; it was really strong. It wasn't gross, but it definitely made me want her again, and I needed to leave soon, so I gave her 'the sign', i.e. I caught her eye, looked at my crotch, back at her and wiggled my eyebrows. She climbed on top and pulled off my shirt. She purred with delight at my chest, and gave it a little rub. I pulled down my pants and kicked them off; she went to take off her shorts and I stopped her, pulled the leg to the side and pulled her onto me. She was so wet, and I thought that maybe she liked the new assertive me. I had the idea that I would stand up

84

while we were fucking, carry her to the kitchen bench, and finish up there. I guess I was feeling confident from before. I'd been strong and she'd loved it. I did everything in the wrong order. I know that now, after having years to reflect on it, and countless times to practice it on others. In my rush, I lifted her, too forcefully as I was getting up, and it lifted her clean off my dick. Then, I struggled to get up from the low couch, so she just fell back down... on my dick... with her anus.

For an instant I had no idea. I was just embarrassed that my plan had gone awry, and I wanted to pretend that I'd meant to just lift her up and put her down. Then, she screamed, punched me in the cheekbone, dug her fingers under my collarbones for leverage, and flew off me, clutching at her ass. She ran around, back and forth for a few seconds, crying and cursing me. Then, she stopped, looked at me through eye slits and hissed 'get out.' She pointed at the door. 'Get. Out.' I was still too stunned to move, so she grabbed my clothes, and started whipping me with them, screaming like a banshee, 'GETOUTGETOUTGETOUT!'

So I got out, and, face against her front door, with my bare and newly hairless ass to the street I pulled on my pants and begged her to calm down. She did not. She called me an ass rapist, a fuckwit, a pervert and more. She told me I was never welcome there again, and that we were done. I asked her if she could please give me my phone, as it had fallen out of my pants when she was lashing me. She reefed the door open, and threw it right past me into the street. I heard it smash and immediately knew Ellison would be infuriated. The door slammed, I shrugged on my shirt and picked up my brand new phone. The screen was well smashed, spidered all over the place. It still worked though, and was in one piece so I figured I could get it repaired, maybe before Ellison found out. I set off to get ready for work.

I never thought I'd feel so glad to put on that little bum bag. I pulled up to work, took a deep breath and strode in, like I'd never been gone. The smell hit me like someone threw a salami cloak over me. It was SO meaty in there. It wasn't revolting, but I didn't want to eat it like I usually did upon my first whiff each shift. They were totally fine, but worried about me. I told them I was out of town and in an accident, that I'd sustained a head injury and they had to keep me for observation. Conveniently my phone had been smashed in the accident, which is why nobody'd heard from me. Blah blah glad you're ok, blah blah can you fill up the pizza bench, blah can you deliver this pizza, blah here's your pay and I was finished. Outside, Ellison was leaning against my car.

'How was work?'

'Fine. What're you doing here?'

'Hello to you too.'

'Ugh. Hello. Why are you here?'

'I smell pussy on you. Who'd you fuck?'

'What? Nobody... what?'

'Fine, lie. I'll get it out of you later.' She arched her back and stretched.

'Why are you here, Ellison?'

She lay on my bonnet. 'I'm ordering a pizza.'

'You don't eat pizza.'

'Yeah but you do.'

'I don't want any pizza, I'm getting Maccas and going home, to MY home.'

She sat up, quicker than she should have. 'Oh, is that a fact?'

'Well...'

'Well?'

I looked into the distance, too scared to look at her. 'C'mon Ellison, I need a rest, I only just got back into the swing of things...'

'Here's the thing, Ulysses,' she inspected her fingernails, 'you don't make the rules, and I don't care what kind of swings you're in. I have a job to do with you. I need to train you, you're my responsibility, remember? We need to find you a job.'

'I have a job,' I jerked my head behind me, 'and I'm already good at it.'

Then, her hand was around my neck and she was whispering in my ear. 'My patience has run out. Get in the car and drive to my place. Now.' She lingered on my neck, squeezing harder for just a moment.

As she let go, I jerked away to let her know that I had her number and I got into the driver's seat. 'Can I at least get food?'

'Maybe. Drive.'

We approached McDonald's and I quietly asked her if I could please get something to eat; I was starving. She nodded, and I pulled in. For the first time ever, I found myself looking at the chicken burgers. I never ate chicken at Maccas, it was Big Mac all the way, baby. This time though, after smelling the ham at Vicki's, and all the salami and crap at work, the thought of meat grossed me out and the least offensive was chicken. Ellison made no comment about my choice and when I asked her if she wanted anything (to be polite, I'm not stupid), she just raised an eyebrow at me. We drove back to her place in silence, except for the time she told me I was chewing like a drunk pirate with no teeth.

Her place was exactly as I remembered, which was a bit of a bummer. I was kinda hoping I had imagined at least some of it. She told me to sit on the couch, so I did. She sat in her power chair and pulled it over in front of me.

'Have you noticed any changes?'

'I only left yesterday.'

'So you haven't?'

'Actually I have...'

Surprisingly, she smirked, and then sat there staring at me with arches for eyebrows.

'Oh, you want me to show you?' I stood up and took off my shirt. She leaned back in the chair and took me in, hand on her chin.

'Is it just your chest?'

I pulled down my pants, mooned her then flashed her. I made my dick give a little wiggle; I don't know why.

'That's happening pretty fast; I'm pleased. And, you actually look a tiny bit more toned.'

'I know, right?' I tensed my biceps, then gave my dwindling man boobs a little jiggle.

'Is that Vicki I smell?'

'What? Waddaya mean?' I threw my shirt back on.

'Don't play coy. I don't care if you fucked her, it's not like I can catch anything.'

'Well, she came onto me, you know.'

'And I bet you fucked her like you never have before.'

'Actually... yes. Is that a vampire thing?'

She shrugged. 'Maybe. You shouldn't be that much stronger or fitter yet. I'd say it was more to do with the fact that you've been through an intense experience and have been my bitch for a week. Were you super dominant?'

'Well, I dunno...'

'Do you think I would allow you to fuck me the way you fucked her?'

'Hell no.'

'Then you were dominant. Good for you. Let's get to work.'

'I accidentally fucked her in the ass.' I immediately wondered why I told her that.

'How do you accidentally do that?'

'I tried to lift her up while I was fucking her. I lifted her, but I couldn't lift myself off the couch, and, well, she came back down on the wrong hole.'

'Was she displeased?'

'Very. She called me an ass rapist and told me to never come back.'

'I'm sorry to hear that.'

'She also threw my phone and broke it.'

'Ugh. Humans. I'll get it fixed. Now, enough about buttertooth. Did you notice anything else?'

'Buttertooth? If I didn't know better, I'd say you were jealous.'

'You obviously don't know better about my patience, because it is getting thin.'

'Ok fine. What else did I notice...' I yawned and stretched. 'Oh, I went into the fish shop yesterday, you know, to return my fish...'

'It was still alive?'

'I know, right? What a trooper! Anyhow, when I was in there, two things happened. One, I crept up on the girl without realising, and two, all of the fish were scared of me, except the real badass ones.'

She crossed her legs under in the chair, and I marvelled at how she could fold up so well. 'That's good progress, actually. The fact that they were scared of you shows that they could sense you were a predator, so you're obviously already changing on a molecular level. The fact that you crept up on her... we'll work on that. How was the sun?'

'Bright, but not too bad. I think it was just cos I'd been here in the dark for so long. What happens when you go in the sun?'

'I get burnt. Very quickly in comparison to humans, but I also recover more quickly. Now, shut up and listen. We need to begin training you up for... whatever it is that you'll end up doing.' She eyed me what I thought was dubiously, like she didn't believe I would be good at anything. I didn't particularly disagree.

'Ok, I'm ready. Are we gunna fight?'

'What? That would be like a grown bear fighting a human baby, you idiot. The first thing is that you need another history lesson. You'll never understand the importance of keeping our existence a secret until you properly understand.'

'Oh, ok. I'm all ears.'

'So. The reason that we may only hunt with a licence is?'

'Because otherwise we would run out of food.'

'Correct. So, how do you think we make sure we get the food we need?'

I frowned, hoping it would make me look like I was thinking hard about the answer. I had no idea.

'Fine, pretend to ponder it, asshole. I'll just tell you. We can't go willy-nilly killing whoever we like. We need to make sure that most babies grow into children, most children grow into adults and that all socio-economic levels are represented.'

'Why? The last part, I mean.'

'Because when people go missing and die, it can't be noticeably from just one major group. We need to ensure that we farm a wide variety of societal types, so that when we harvest, it seems random.'

I had a sudden thought. 'Is it also because some people taste better, depending on what they eat? I know Vic asked me once to eat more pineapple so that my-'

'No, dipshit,' she cut me off. 'Blood is blood. It tastes... better... richer if it is nice and healthy is all, but we can survive on blood from even the sick and dying, unless they are really far gone. If that's the case then that blood won't get us too far. It's like if a human ate nothing but two minute noodles. There's no sustenance there. Dealers mix all sorts of blood together so that there is a wide range for everyone's budget.'

'What, so, like you might mix a really old man dying of cancer with some fresh young athlete to make it more affordable?'

'Pretty much, yes.'

'I have questions.' I got a sudden rush of assertiveness and I got up and began to pace, hand on my chin to show I was in thought. I felt stupid, and dropped it to my side. She watched me with what seemed like a smile, though I never really knew with her.

'Alright, then ask.'

'How do you pick who dies?'

'It's done with a sort-of-a formula, to make it seem random.'

'Why?'

'Because most humans believe in a god, and they believe that when someone young is taken suddenly, that it is the will of that god, and they don't question it.'

'What about people who don't believe in god?'

'They're smart enough to know that life is random, death is random. They know there is no particular rhyme or reason to life. They try to keep themselves healthy for the most part, to give themselves the best chance at a long life, but when they go, they go, and they accept it as the random chaos that is life.'

I reached the end of the room, and realised that the windows weren't entirely blacked out. At night time, I could see the lights of the city, just subdued. It was beautiful and I felt sort-of peaceful, for the first time in ages. 'But if we can choose who we take, then why not take all the baddies?'

'Ulysses. Think about what you're saying. You're smarter than that. What would happen if we only took bad people?'

'There would be less crime and killing and stuff?'

'Exactly. So how would that affect us, and our way of life?'

'It would be less competition for you?'

'For us.'

'For us.'

'More to the point, it would mean fewer ways for us to hide.'

'Why?'

She sighed. 'Think about it, Ulysses–'

'You can call me Uly.'

She glared at me. 'Think about it Uly,' she still stared at me, and I assumed she was willing me to interrupt again; I didn't. 'If we only killed,' she motioned air quotes, '"baddies", then there would be far lower crime rates, that's true. That would be good for our consciences, make us feel as if we had a higher purpose as righteous vigilantes, picking up where the justice system left off, right? There are downsides to that though, for example when all the "baddies" are being killed, panic would rise about vigilantes, which would work against our secret, and when they're all gone, potential "baddies" would be deterred, meaning that all crime would dry up. This would throw everything into imbalance. Where would all the prison guards work? What would police do? Where would all the jobs come from if all these would-be criminals suddenly had to earn their living honestly? It would just give rise to poverty. The nation and the world would begin to crumble. Also, how would we harvest our food if we had no regular crime to camouflage our crime?'

'I never thought about it like that.'

'Of course you didn't, you've never had to before. What's more, if we didn't kill a certain amount of infants and young people, then the population would grow out of control.'

I looked down at the lights and thought about what she'd said. I imagined people wandering around down there in the darkness, unaware that they were possibly the target for some vampire's next meal, unaware that they may be about to die just so that the 'random' nature of it all is upheld. People tucking their kids into bed for the last time, totally oblivious that in the morning that kid would be lying there dead, all part of vampires' master plan. 'That's all a bit shit.'

'Yeah, it is. But, that's life.'

I thought of another question. 'But don't people get suspicious when corpses are drained of all their blood?'

'We don't drain them, just take a couple of litres, and sometimes people just go missing, never to be seen again. Then we can drain them. We've been doing this for thousands upon thousands of years, it works pretty well.'

'Hm.'

'Hm indeed. Got any more questions for now?'

I turned to look at her, still in her chair, still sitting lotus style, still looking directly into my soul. 'No, I'm all questioned out. Got any pizza leftover?'

'Have a seat; I'll get it for you.' Surprised at her hospitality, I shuffled to the couch in a bit of a daze, and flopped into the familiar cushioning. I thought about my old life and the blissful ignorance I'd unknowingly enjoyed. I missed it.

She handed me the pizza and without really registering what I was doing, I picked all of the ham,

discovery when some rice, berries and honey sat around rotting after a human (unknowingly of course) gave them as a gift to a vampire. In an effort to maintain the charade, upon a surprise visit by a human, the vampire prepared a meal as best he could, and he noticed that after consuming the food, the human became unsteady, pliable and quite jolly. With the passage of time, and after further consumption, the human became all but completely incapacitated. As the story goes, the vampire killed him, had a feast of his own and began to deliberately ferment different things in an effort to come up with a substance that humans would willingly ingest, leading to much easier killings. Thus, alcohol was born. Now, here's the clincher: vampires own all the major alcohol companies over the whole globe. Even if stupid humans ever did get to a point where they realised that alcohol is dangerous and ruins bodies and lives and they tried to make it illegal, they would fail, because vampires have the monopoly on that. Why, you ask? Because it causes human deaths and provides more cover for vampire harvesting. How many automotive deaths are associated with alcohol? How many party mishaps? How many miserable people drowning their sorrows? What's that? Procreation is a little slow for the past few years? Encourage more drinking. Drunk = fuck = babies. It's the same with tobacco. Remember I said before that vampires don't really care what kind of blood they have, as long as the human isn't 'too far gone'? Someone dying of lung cancer or emphysema looks like crap anyway, nobody's going to notice if a litre of blood goes missing now and then. They sneak in like rats in the night and take it, while the human is fucking dying. When they hit their last month or so, the vampires let them be, leave them to die with their useless weak blood. So, cigarettes contribute to the great cause in that way, and also because cigarettes encourage alcohol consumption, and vice versa. Those two legal drugs work hand-in-hand to do their part to keep the vampire population thriving the world over. Shitty, huh?

I was getting sleepy on the couch, so my questions became a little less valid. 'Do vampires smoke and drink?'

'Mostly the ones who did as humans, because they miss it. They love to smoke in particular, because it isn't dangerous for them, so the guilt disappears. It can be a very handy way to meet people: outside clubs in the smoking area, beer gardens etc. Sometimes non-smoking harvesters will smoke if it helps them to fit in with a targeted human. Drinking they tend to hold onto less. Our bodies are too efficient to allow any effects from the alcohol, and if their drink of choice was bourbon and coke for example, then eventually the sugar will just make them sick. Some end up drinking things like fine whisky, neat, for years after they were made, but they're mostly pompous assholes.'

'This is all so fucked up.'

'Yeah.'

And then I slept.

I woke up at 5:30am. That was very odd for me. I wondered what had woken me. I looked around. Ellison was standing at the window, naked. It seemed like she was just watching the streets. Any noises I heard were muffled and subdued. I didn't need to pee.

As far as I could tell, I just woke up because my body was done resting; I was wide awake. I didn't even feel that groggy. I sat up and gave my hairless balls a good scratch. The leftover pizza sat beside the couch still. I opened it and stared at the grease-soaked napkin covering the tiny pork cadaver. I couldn't do it; I closed the lid. It was official, I was grossed out by pork.

'What's happening to me? I used to love bacon...'

She turned, and I took in her body. Each time I saw it, it was like a new time, as if I'd forgotten how sexy she was. The windows let in a little bit of light through the heavy tinting and she was rosy where it had sat on her skin. She leaned against the window and watched me watch her.

'Why are you naked? Are we going to have sex?'

'Ulysses, we are nowhere near the day when I will allow you to initiate sex. I am naked because after hundreds of years the shame surrounding my naked body has disappeared. Like so many other societal rules, it no longer applies to me. I'm not wearing clothes because I don't need to. And, you are evolving; you don't need to eat pork anymore. Your body is becoming better, more efficient and it's telling you that you feel sick every time you see, smell or taste pork, because it doesn't want you to put that shit in your body.'

'Will it just be pork?'

'Do you listen to me at all? Eventually you won't need to consume anything but human blood, and anything but blood will make you sick.'

I looked at my wrist, and saw the little blue snakes, still there under my skin. 'Will I just... all of a sudden... crave blood?' I expected her to snap at me for the stupid question.

'I'm not going to snap at you, that's actually a fair question. No you won't, actually. You'll have to wean yourself onto it like if you suddenly decided to start eating a new food that previously grossed you out.'

'Um, what?'

'What? It makes sense. You're gradually going off your food already. In a week or two we'll start trying you with blood.'

'What... like... from a person?'

'Yep. We'll get someone in here, a vagrant maybe... get him under the pretence of a hot shower and meal. We'll wash him, then I'll incapacitate him and you can bite his neck.'

I leapt to my feet. 'What?!? I'm not ready for that!'

'Good, because I'm being facetious. If you drank that much blood at once you would be violently ill. Also, humanoid teeth are very ineffective at tearing flesh.'

I was intently aware of my heart pounding. I wanted to punch her tits off. Making fun of me when I'm already confused, what a bitch...

'I heard that.'

'Well, that was uncool... How will I do it then?'

'In milk.'

'Milk?'

'Yes. It's a beverage that's quite acceptable to humans to drink, so I imagine you're used to it. It's the only bodily fluid you have ever taken a full drink of, I imagine.'

'So, are we gunna... like, put a bit of blood in a glass of milk?'

'Precisely. See, you are smarter than you look. Get yourself some cornflakes; they're in the cupboard.'

She was right. There was a box of cornflakes and nothing else. In the fridge among the stacked bags was a carton of milk. I pulled it out and set it on the counter. Then, I opened the fridge again and grabbed out the first bag I saw. I turned it over in my hands. It was weightier than I thought it would be; it felt sort-of hefty. I watched it pour around as I moved it. I didn't feel any pull to it. I decided to smell it, and before Ellison could get there, I popped the top off one of the two little tubes coming from it. I was already lowering my nose to it, so when I inadvertently squeezed it from just the pressure of holding it, the force was great enough to squirt it directly up my right nostril. I must have gasped in surprise, because it shot down the back of my throat and also out of my mouth. I dropped the bag; Ellison caught it, recapped it and tossed it in the sink as I was still collapsing to my knees. I coughed and spluttered and sneezed; blood was everywhere. Even though I was fully aware that it wasn't my blood, something in me still felt panicked at the sight of it all, coming from my head. I was surprised to find that it tasted like my own blood. At that thought, I began to gag. I tried to get up and

102

slipped in it; both my arms shot to my right, and I face planted the bloody tiles with my forehead. Instantly, my head throbbed and I just lay there for a few seconds, my eyes shut. When I opened them, she was standing over me. She had a curious expression on her face. She didn't seem angry, though she was frowning at me. All of a sudden, she burst into laughter. I'd never seen her smile when she wasn't being evil at me. Her smile was pretty, and it caught me off guard.

'I'm sorry! I didn't mean to do that!' I scrambled to get up again, slipped around like a baby deer and eventually managed to find my feet. I stood in front of her. She was still chuckling.

'You are completely useless!' She cracked up some more.

I looked down at myself. Somebody I didn't know had their blood all over my shirt, my pants and the floor. It looked like someone had been stabbed to death. How much did I squirt up there?

'Wait here and take off your clothes.' She walked towards the shower. I did as I was told, too stunned to say anything smarmy in return. I did figure it was sex time, though. She came back with a towel and threw it at me. 'Make sure you don't walk any to the shower.'

By the time I was clean, the horror had subsided, and I was keen for the cornflakes. Ellison was back in her chair, cross-legged and wearing jeans and a shirt. I spoke from the kitchen, preparing my corny feast.

'Why'd you put clothes on?'

'Two reasons: one, so you can tell when it might be sex time or not, and two, because we're going out.'

'Where're we going?'

'You'll see.' I don't know why I expected her to be any less mysterious all of a sudden. I brought my flakes to the couch.

'I kinda thought that maybe you would've wanted to have sex in all that blood...'

'Why?'

'I dunno... I thought that's what vampires did...'

'It's my food, and my business. Thrashing about in it would be nothing but a waste. Also, it stains things. Would you want to fuck in your cornflakes?'

'Hm. Point taken.'

'Hurry up.' So, she was back to being moody.

'What happens if a vampire doesn't wean onto blood?'

She stretched, which I hadn't seen her do before. 'One of a few things. Sometimes new vampires think they can keep eating regular food, so they persevere and miss their window to get used to blood. Then it comes to a point where they need it very bad, but their stomach rejects it and they become very ill. Sometimes, they die. Sometimes, they don't. Sometimes, they're stubborn and simply do not give in. Then, they starve to death. Then, there are a few who think they can survive on animal blood.'

'Can they?'

'Not for very long. They lead half-lives... they're weak and not much good to anyone. They burn very easily and can get infections and die that way. They heal slowly. They're the exception to immortality, really. I've never heard of one living longer than five, six hundred years.'

'What a bummer...'

'Bummer indeed. Put shoes on.' She headed for the door.

'I'm not finished my flakes!'

'Learn to eat quicker,' she shot over her shoulder. 'Do not make me wait for you.'

I crammed my mouth full, shoved my feet in my shoes and stumbled out after her.

I was wondering how we were going to do this, since it was daytime. As it turned out, Ellison had picked the time just right, because from the front door of her building to the subway, it was shaded. We rode in silence; I was still hungry and miffed about it. We got off at the station under the mall and I was quite impressed. We could spend hours in there, until nightfall if we wanted. I looked at her; she was wearing a mask of smug so I kept my comments to myself. Then, I realised she probably knew them anyway and I was irritated. I heard her chuckle. She led me to the food court and sat at a table. Theatrically, she waved her hand to indicate the culinary wonders of the food court, and I understood.

Back at our table where only one of us was eating, she finally spoke. 'Do you know why we're here?'

In between chewing: 'No.'

'We're here to begin your training, and to see how far you've progressed.'

'To see if I'm stronger yet?'

She sighed. I knew that sigh. I was irritating her. 'If you are referring to physical strength, then you will most likely be disappointed. You will only ever notice a *slight* increase in strength and fitness unless you really work at it.'

'Oh what? Why?'

'Because being a vampire is not magic. Like any bodybuilder, you would have to work at it if you wanted to get huge. The difference between a huge you and a huge human is that if you both ceased working out, it would take a much, much longer time for you to lose your form, because your body would be better at holding it once you got it to that point, understand?'

I nodded.

'So if you do nothing but your usual walking around, going to the toilet and delivering pizzas, then your body as a vampire will reach a decent enough state, and that is all. But, that state would be much fitter than a human who did the same level of exercise. Get it?'

More nodding.

'Ulysses-'

'Uly.'

More sighing. 'Ulysses', I didn't choose you for your bodyguard potential; I chose you because you're a douche. I'm sick of creating bleeding hearts and suffering through their conscience woes. You don't have to work out if you don't want, unless you want to be a bodyguard. If that is the case, you will become huge very quickly, and I won't stop you. All I need to do is get you to a point where you are supporting yourself and contributing to vampire society.'

I wiped pizza sauce off my chin. 'I don't wanna be a bodyguard. I hate working out.'

She eyed me. 'I figured. Pizza?!? Again?!?'

I looked at it. It was one of those gourmet types, with fetta and spinach... and no meat.

'No meat, eh?' She winked; I took another bite.

'What I am hoping, is that we will at least be able to develop your psychological strengths, so you have some form of self-defence.'

'So, that stuff doesn't come naturally either?'

She put her head in her hands. 'Goddammit. No. Aspects of your body—the senses that you already had—will be enhanced over time, as your new biology hones you like a machine. You'll see perfectly, hear perfectly and you'll probably never lose your voice again. You'll very rarely, if ever get sick. You'll recover from injury very fast, and be able to recover from things that no human body could withstand, if we can get you to care in time. But, skills that you don't already have, like telekinesis and mind control will have to be realised, taught. And, I'm sure—well I hope—that it goes without saying, any skills you develop as a vendor or a harvester will also need to be taught to you.'

'By you?'

'Psychological stuff and vending, yes. Harvesting, no. I am not a harvester.'

'Ok, well I'm ready. Where do we start?'

She took my paper plate, sat it in the middle of the table. 'The aim is for you to move this plate, with your mind. Look at the plate and only the plate. Do not look at me. I am going to continue talking to you, and to everyone else it will look like we are simply having a conversation. I brought you here deliberately because it is loud. If you can do it here, then we can skip all the easy stuff.'

'So, what... I'm just gunna stare at it and it'll move?'

'No, dick. Staring is staring. Let me finish.'

'Yeah alright. Jeez...'

'Focus on the plate and nothing else. Let all the noise of the mall fade into the background. Let it be a radio on low volume in the next room. Notice the plate. Notice the shape of it, the colour of it, the ridges and the stains left by the pizza. Really examine the plate. Your mind will try to think of other things and pull you away; don't let it. Stay with the plate. Now, while your mind is focusing only on the plate, I want you to picture it moving a centimetre to the left, your left. Picture the plate there, the same as it is, just a centimetre to the left...'

She went silent, and I did everything she told me. One second I was staring at the plate, then it flew into my face. I got a fright, let out a startled 'oh!' and batted at it, like it was attacking me. It fluttered to the floor. I looked at Ellison. Her face was distorted because she was trying not to bust out into laughter at me; I knew that look anywhere. I wasn't mad though. I grinned at her and she let it out; threw her head back and guffawed. She composed herself, picked up a napkin and swabbed at my face where the plate had left sauce.

She took a deep breath. 'Well, it's definitely there, just needs some fine-tuning...'

I picked up the plate. 'Ya think? Try again?'

'No... let's try something more fun... go get yourself a coffee and get an extra cup and lid.'

'Please wouldn't go astray...'

'Please.'

I was still as mesmerised as ever by the smell of freshly brewed coffee. I wanted a latte but thought about all the milk, and then the blood all over the floor. I willed the thought away and ordered.

As I returned, she got up. 'Come this way.' She led us to a bench facing a thoroughfare and several shops. 'Sit.'

I sat beside her and handed her the empty cup and lid. She put the lid on and pretended to drink. Of course. She even swallowed; I was inwardly impressed.

'Now, you're going to try it on a person.'

'Oh what?'

'Relax, it'll be fine. It's much harder than making a paper plate fly into your own face...'

'Ugh. Fine. What do I do?'

'See that guy over there?' She pointed to a man walking with a woman and a kid. They were just strolling, the adults chatting, the little girl making a huge mess with an ice cream in a cone.

'Yeah.'

'Look at him, and do the same stuff you were doing with the paper plate. Try to make one of his legs take a step to either side. Oh, I almost forgot. Here.' She handed me a pair of sunnies.

I put them on and stared. His legs were moving, so it was hard to concentrate like I did on the plate. I decided to try his arms instead; he wasn't really swinging them. The more I concentrated on them, the weirder they looked, two big heavy lifeless eels just dangling at his sides. I focused on the right one. It immediately shot out and slapped the ice cream from the little girl's hands. It flew over the railing to the floor below; I heard a shout. The guy was stunned. The little girl paused, then burst into tears. The guy looked at his hand and then to the woman, who was open-mouthed staring at him and shaking her head. He crouched in front of the kid and I heard him apologise and promise her another.

'Oh my god. Oh my god. Was that you?' Ellison was grinning, hiding it behind her coffee cup.

'I... I think so?'

'I said legs!'

'I know, but they were moving too much!'

'Try the legs! Idiot!'

'Yeah alright,' I grumbled and focused on the left one. They were heading for the food court; the little girl was rubbing her eyes with one hand, holding her Dad's hand with the other. I really stared at that left leg, and got used to the rhythm of him walking. Suddenly, I felt a connection, and mid-stride, I froze his leg. As a consequence, he missed that step, but his body kept going with the right leg. There was no left leg to counter balance, and he completely face planted. He was holding hands with the woman and the girl! The woman shook him off like he was a poisonous spider; the little girl went down with him. Both of them spudded into the carpet with their actual faces. She was howling, the woman was yelling and he was scrambling to get up, pick the girl up and figure out what the hell happened.

'Oh!' I whispered, 'oh no!'

'Oh my god. We need to go.' Still stifling laughter behind an empty coffee cup, she got up and headed back to the food court.

Directly in front of us was Manny.

He didn't see me at first; he seemed to be staring into the distance. He was with a man I didn't recognise, who was facing the food court. I stopped.

'Manny?'

He snapped to look at me and for a second looked like he was terrified. Then, recognition washed over him and he relaxed. 'Hey man, what's up? Gunna introduce me to your lady friend?' He twisted his hands like he was nervous, but I'd never known him to be, so I wasn't really sure.

It was my turn to be terrified. What if Manny recognised Ellison? This shit was about to get weird. She turned to look at him with that Cheshire Cat smile. I knew that smile; she was gunna slack-face him. Instead, he stood up, reached out his hand and introduced himself and the smile drained down her face, leaving anger in its wake. Still, she smiled, exchanged pleasantries and grasped my arm so hard I knew it would bruise.

'Hello, Dragomir,' she purred.

Manny's man friend spun around a little too fast, but remained seated. His voice was like a snake's hiss; exactly how you'd expect a vampire to sound. 'Hello, Ellison.' He spat her name like it was bitter candy. 'What brings you here?'

'The same as you, it seems.'

'Hm.' He eyed me up and down, with an expression like he was still sucking on that bitter candy.

I looked at Manny, but he was looking at the floor.

'Well, lovely to meet you, Manny, but we have errands. Until next time, Dragomir...' she jerked me by the arm and I tripped and stumbled after her, like her cavorting lap dog.

'What the hell was that?' I hissed when we were a good hundred metres away.

'That,' she pulled me to face her, 'was Dragomir and his newest companion.'

'Manny?!?' I indicated back with my thumb. 'Are you telling me Manny is a vampire?'

'That's exactly what I'm telling you, and his creator is an absolute asshole.'

'How could you tell?'

'Well, for a start, he was practicing like you were when we walked up. Also, when I tried to enter his mind, it was completely different from the other night, much harder.'

'Did this guy pick him because of me? Because he's my friend?'

'Doubtful, but with Dragomir you never know...'

'What's with than name, anyway? Dragomir? What's with vampires and weird names?'

'Ellison was the name I was given at my human birth, jerk. Dragomir chose his name when he became a vampire. It means "precious peace".' She theatrically rolled her eyes. 'He is *such* a douche.'

'Do you, like, have a history with him?'

She looked at me blankly, so I made a ring shape with one hand, and inserted my finger into it several times, rapidly. She simply raised an eyebrow. 'I don't think so, though he did try.' We began to walk again, towards the subway.

'Manny... wow... I feel like he's just gunna fuck lots of chicks if he can get good at mind control... that's kinda messed up...'

Ellison chuckled. 'Dragomir doesn't allow his creations to have sex with others...'

'You mean...'

'Uh-huh. Manny is officially homosexual, for the next hundred years at least.'

'But Manny isn't gay.'

'He is now.'

She jumped the turnstile, and I walked right into it.

Chapter Eight

Manny, a vampire? When? He seemed like regular old Manny the night of my birthday: an arrogant womaniser. When he came to my place yesterday, he did seem weird, but I thought he was genuinely confused about being slack-faced. Was he lying? Testing me? Today he seemed positively terrified to see me. Once again, we rode the subway in silence, and I thought of all the horror movies and TV shows I'd seen featuring vampires living in the underground railway tunnels. I looked out the window but saw only darkness rushing by. My mind slipped back to Manny, taking it in the ass for a hundred years. He loved women so much. This might just kill him.

It was still daylight as we walked back to Ellison's place. We walked side-by-side: me in the sun, her in the shade. To this day, I don't know what possessed me to do it, but I slid my hand into hers. For the tiniest of moments, I thought she was going to let it happen. Then she jerked her hand out and punched me in the jaw with it. We walked the rest of the way with no touching.

She let me go to work that night, but told me to come back to her place to sleep.

Work was work, but the smell of all the meat was getting a bit tedious. I took more deliveries than usual, keen to get out of there. As my shift drew to a close, I realised I felt restless. I didn't want to go straight back to Ellison's. I wanted some space to think, to breathe. I wanted to talk to Manny. I wanted to practice my new skills more.

I decided not to tell her. I just finished my shift, locked up my car and started walking. It took thirteen minutes for her first text to arrive.

'It's been enough time. Where r u?'

'Going for a walk. I'll be there later.'

'No. Come now.'

'No.'

'Ulysses, I'm serious. Do not make me come and get you.'

'Ugh just chill, E. It's only a walk. Maybe a drink, maybe a little "skills" practice, whatever. I need some time to think.'

'Under NO CIRCUMSTANCES are you to practice ANYTHING without me present!!'

I was getting mad. I'd lost so much over the last two weeks; I was craving some independence. I was sick to death of being somebody's bitch. This was why I didn't do girlfriends.

'Sick of being your little BITCH. I need a night off. I'll be there when I'm fucking there.'

I text Manny: 'Obvs we need to talk. You free?'

I walked for a half hour, receiving no texts from anybody. I don't know if it was intentional or not, but suddenly I found myself looking up at that softly buzzing BA sign; I went inside.

I ordered a bourbon and coke, but it tasted too acidic, so I ordered a bourbon on the rocks, which was better. I asked the bartender about my jacket. He told me he didn't know what I was talking about. As if scripted, his offsider came in from the cellar (stage left) wearing my fucking jacket.

'Dude. That's my jacket.'

'Clearly not, as I'm wearing it.'

'Yeah but you obviously found it here when I fucking left it here last week.'

'So you say.'

'I do say, motherfucker, and I want it back.'

'Then come and take it.'

I figured it was my cue. I stared at him hard, trying to focus like I had in the mall. He frowned.

'What are you doing?'

Undaunted, I stared harder; I felt myself tremble a little.

'What the fuck? What are you doing you fucking freak?'

I was trying so hard to slack-face him but I didn't know how. I focused on his right arm instead, and he immediately punched himself in the face. He stumbled backwards and went wild-eyed. He staggered towards the bar and I tried to do it again. Instead he grandly swept everything off the counter with his possessed arm. Glasses shattered and tinkled in all directions, and every eye in the place turned to him. He was frozen in place: not because of me, because he was scared, and I knew he was scared. I mean, I didn't just assume it by collating all the social cues and my knowledge of human behaviour. I could feel it. It rolled off him like his own personal fog. I couldn't see it, but it was there. It didn't smell, but I could taste it, sort-of inside my head. It was sharp but sweet, not unlike an armpit. He made eye contact with me; I didn't break it. I concentrated harder than ever, visualising his right arm reaching to his left cuff. His right arm began to move. I knew it was me, because his head snapped to look at it, and his fear fog knocked up a notch. Somehow, I could feel his right arm, as if it were mine, but in addition to mine, if that makes sense. He frantically looked back at me, panic creeping into his fear. His right arm tugged at his left cuff, but because I couldn't control the left at the same time, nothing happened except for the increasingly violent tugging. He madly shook his left arm, presumably in an effort to rid it of the right, but that just added to the mix; he was really starting to alarm people. I stopped controlling his arm. He didn't react in time, so as his right arm fell by his side, he spun around, jerking at thin air with the left, slipped in all the spilled alcohol and crashed to the floor. He scrambled to get up, but kept putting his hands in glass, only to snatch them up in pain and immediately try again. I stood up, peering over the bar at him.

'Looks like my jacket doesn't suit you so well...'

He stopped moving, looked at me and then whipped it off.

'Take the fucking thing! It's ugly anyway!' He threw it in my face but I snatched it out of the air before it could hit me.

'Thanks, mate. Appreciate it.' I flashed him my toothiest grin, shrugged it on, grabbed my bourbon and headed for a booth. I couldn't believe it. Sure, it'd been messy, and it wasn't actually my control that physically removed the jacket, but in the end it worked. For the first time in what felt like forever, I felt like a man, the master of my own destiny and I liked it.

No sooner had my ass hit the seat, my phone buzzed; it was Manny.

'Dragomir gone to work. I got a few hours. Where?'

'Ba?'

'Be there in 10.'

Still nothing from Ellison. I had assumed she would have downloaded an app to trace my phone, or something, but I guessed I was wrong, since she hadn't shown up. I thought maybe she was real mad, or even white-hot mad and at that moment she was actively plotting my demise. Either way, I thought, right now I'm a fucking boss.

Since I was facing the door, I recognised Manny the second he slunk in. It was bizarre. Usually he was so cocky and strutted in like he owned the place, or at least managed it. But that night he scurried to my booth glancing sideways like he was smuggling home-made booze into the bar. He slipped in to face me, and I don't think I imagined him wince when he sat.

For a long moment we just looked at one another, then I broke the silence.

'When did he turn you?'

'Your birthday.'

I was stunned and couldn't hide it; I felt my mouth hang open. I closed it then opened it again to speak but nothing came out. He was silent also, and we just looked at each other for a minute. He actually looked pretty good, healthy. I couldn't stand it anymore so I started my long list of questions.

'Why did you come to see me? Why did you lie to me?'

'I came around to see if Dragomir was lying. He told me that he saw you leave with another vampire, a woman... I just had a feeling... that it was her.'

'But why'd you lie? Why'd you tell me you didn't remember what happened?'

'To an extent, I don't. Dragomir filled me in. I figured that if she got to you, turned you, then you wouldn't in a million years think I was a vampire too, and that you'd lie to me about what happened. If not, and you were none the wiser, you'd tell me that I walked over to her, dumped a drink on my own head and then left the bar in a trance.'

'So... you wanted to see if I had been made a vampire or not?'

'Yes.'

'Why didn't you just tell me that you were too, when you realised?'

'Dragomir told me not to.'

'Why?'

'I don't know. What I do know is that when I break his rules, it doesn't work out well for me, so...'

I decided, since we were being brutally honest, that I'd just cut to the chase. 'Ellison says Dragomir is gay.'

'He's more like bisexual. He's gay this century.'

It burst from my mouth like a cat from a box. 'Does he fuck you in the ass?'

'Way more than I'd like, but yes.'

'Wait, there's an amount that you'd like? Is it zero?'

'Uly, there's no point bothering to hide it anymore, not with you anyway. I'm gay.'

My mouth hung open yet again.

'I've known since I was ten.'

I threw back the rest of my drink; it didn't touch the sides.

'My family... coming out just wasn't an option... so I fucked chicks for show, and fucked guys for fun.'

'But you love chicks.'

'Nope. I love getting my dick sucked. If I close my eyes and picture it's a dude, it's almost as good. I hardly ever fucked them, you know, unless they'd let me do it in the ass. I was so horrible to them for a reason; I hardly ever had to pick up to maintain the front.'

'How did you pick up guys? Where?'

'Anywhere, I'm not fussy. I've had more back-alley sex than you've delivered pizzas, no pun intended, though that too.'

My mind was blown. I went to take another drink, realised it was empty and looked to the bar in time to catch the eye of my jacket thief. I stared him down, held up my glass and pointed to it. He nodded emphatically and set about making me another.

'What's with that?' Manny jerked his head at the bar.

'I had to get a little rough with him earlier. He stole my jacket.'

'Fair enough.'

'So how did you meet Dragomir then?'

'That night, he was in here. He saw Ellison control me; he hates her.'

'Why?'

'He says she tried to crack onto him once, he said no and she got nasty.'

I chuckled. 'She says the same thing, in reverse.'

He cocked his head. 'Zat so? Anyways, he followed me out and trailed me until it wore off. Then, he took over and made me come to his apartment. The rest is history; I imagine much the same as you. I went to your place every day looking for you when he told me that he'd heard Ellison had created that night too.'

'Are you fucking with me?'

'No, that's exactly how it happened.'

'No, not about that. Are you really gay?'

'Yes.'

'You take it in the ass.'

'Yes, and give it.'

'Does it hurt?'

'Yes, but it also feels good.'

'Do you get to fuck Dragomir?'

'No, that's the only shitty part. Right now, I'm purely bottom, and my bottom is seeing a lot of action.'

'Gross.'

'You asked. Does Ellison let you fuck her?'

'No.'

'So you guys don't have sex at all?'

'Yeah, we do, but she rapes me.'

He sat back in his seat. 'What? Waddaya mean rape?'

'I don't wanna fuck her.'

'Why, cos she's chubby?'

'No, what? That's not the issue. Actually I think she's really sexy. I just don't like her.'

'So hate fuck her.'

'She doesn't let me have any control. She just pins me and rides me. I'm not even allowed to touch her. She hits me you know...'

'Least you're not getting fucked in the ass ten times a day.'

'That much?!'

'Sometimes more.'

'I just cannot believe you're gay.'

'I just cannot believe we're vampires.'

My drink arrived. I turned to Manny while my new bitch was still there. 'You want a drink, man? It's on the house.'

'Nah, thanks. I gotta go. If Dragomir finds out I went out, he'll be real mad.'

I shooed the barkeep away. 'Will I see you again?'

He got up and shrugged, 'Probably, who knows? Everything's pretty weird now.'

As he slunk out of the bar, this time it made more sense. He was afraid of Dragomir discovering he was there. I wondered why Dragomir had told Manny not to tell me he was also a vampire.

I sat back in my seat and tried not to think about Ellison. I closed my eyes and tried to really slow down my breathing; I began to relax. It felt good to have some space. I let myself listen to the sounds of the bar and wondered if my hearing had begun to improve. Words and fragments of conversations floated to me and I caught the gist of several different discussions. Maybe I would have been a little sad were it not for the fact that I was still able to get a buzz from alcohol. It was a little depressing to hear all those plans and taste a tiny bit of those friendships, knowing that they were going to be surrounded by loved ones always, but that I would constantly outlive anyone important in my life. I was concentrating on the next table over—two young guys who were trying to drum up the balls to visit a whorehouse—when it began to play. Ob La Di, Ob La Fucking Da. I opened my eyes, turned in my seat and glared at the jukebox. There was nobody near it. I'd always loved that machine. Old school, it still had actual records in it. I stared at it and focused my energy; it helped that I hate that fucking song. I felt myself somehow relax. My stare narrowed and opened up at the same time. I could feel the cool metal of the record player's arm on my fingertips, though I hadn't left my seat. Without moving whatsoever, I slowly and deliberately dragged that arm right across the vinyl. The screech and crackle was both horrid and elating at once. People groaned and some held their ears. The needle reached the edge and there was a moment of silence before conversation recommenced. People assumed that it was a fault with the record, or the player but it was me. I wished that I had the skill to pick the next song, but I was also ecstatic that I'd come as far as I had in just a few days. I was on a high. I downed my drink, left no tip and slid out of the booth. As I passed the bar, the jacket thief stole a glance. I gave him the finger without looking at him, and strode into the cool night air.

I was feeling powerful, drunk though I'd only had the two drinks. I was horny and keen to dominate like

I had with Vic. I was never good-looking enough to be too picky, and since Ellison told me that I wasn't about to suddenly get handsome, I figured nothing would change. I knew where to go. Three blocks from Ba was an area known just as 'the block'. You could get pretty much anything on the block: meth, heroin, shitty quality cocaine, weapons and sex. It was too hardcore for the weed dealers. I'd never spent any time there except when I'd had to pass through but I knew what to look for. Pretty much any lady on the block was looking for some cash. I was getting harder by the second, so literally the first woman to offer me a 'good time' was the winner. She introduced herself as Ruby. She smelled of onions and cheap perfume, was maybe forty and was wearing a tiny red dress. She had a prettiness about her, and I knew she must have a story of promise before the drugs got their hooks in. She dragged me down the nearest alley; I was already unbuttoning my pants. She stopped at a pile of pallets and turned to face me.

'It's fifty bucks to fuck for ten minutes, or until you blow. You only get to blow once. No anal, no kissing. If you only want head, it's thirty, but if you decide you wanna fuck after that, it's another fifty.'

I frantically yanked at my pants for my wallet. I freed it, and immediately dropped it. I grabbed it, and snatched out a hundred bucks.

'Can I come twice for a hundred?'

She chuckled, 'long as it doesn't take more than ten minutes.'

'Oh, it won't.' I dropped my pants to my ankles, spun her around and bent her over the pallets. She was pulling at her underwear, too slow. I grabbed them and shoved them down her legs; I heard a tear. I hoped for her sake she was wet because I was not waiting. I grabbed her hips and pushed inside her, hard. She gasped and I almost came right then. Her skin felt so hot under my hands; I gripped harder and let loose. She was moaning and panting; and the slapping sound was way too loud to be discreet, but I didn't care. I looked up and saw the stars. I thought about how long I was going to be able to look at them, how long I was going to be able to fuck women like this, and I came, so hard that I lifted her off the ground a bit.

I pulled out and turned her around. We were both panting.

'I think I got a splinter,' she huffed, and held her hand in the moonlight to see better. I looked around, pulled up my pants, ran and grabbed a cardboard box from further down the alley. I flattened it and laid it on top of the pallets. She cocked her head at me, and I have to admit, I was surprised too. No matter how many times Ellison fucked me without my consent, I never wanted to get rapey with a chick. I mean, I like it rough, but crying isn't sexy at all. I picked her up, sat her on the pallets and dropped my pants again; I was already hard. She gave a little squeal of delight, opened her legs and I wasted no time. I lasted longer on round two: nowhere near ten minutes, but I don't think she was timing me anyways. I started out slowly, closed my eyes and concentrated on what I could feel. She was so warm, inside and out. Everything felt so vibrant.

'Choke me.'

My eyes snapped open. 'What?'

'Choke me. I like it.'

Without breaking my rhythm, I let go her hips and reached for her neck. Instantly, I felt her pulse; it was so strong and fast. I could feel it with both of my hands. I started to thrust more forcefully.

'Harder,' she whispered.

I didn't know if she meant the choking or the fucking, so I did both. It was glorious. I was so powerful. While pinning her by her neck, I felt her whole body move as I fucked her. I just fucked harder and harder, with her life force in my bare hands. I completely lost myself. I had no concept of time or place, and when I came, it was the hardest I ever had and I cried out like a beast. I was dizzy. I let go of her neck, pulled out and collapsed on the ground. It was cool on my bare ass, and as my breathing slowed, I looked at the stars again and contemplated the pros of being a vampire, no pun intended.

I was enjoying the quiet until I actually realised it was quiet.

'Ruby? You ok? I didn't hurt you, did I? You did ask me to choke you...'

Nothing.

'Ruby?'

I scrambled to get up, but my pants were still around my ankles. I lay back down and pulled them up like a girl putting on skinny leg jeans. I jumped up to find her sprawled on the pallets, staring at the stars and completely limp. Her tongue seemed way too big and was bulging out of her mouth.

'Ruby?' I gently shook her. 'Ruby?' I shook harder. Her head lolled to the side, and even in the darkness I could see her throat was crushed. 'Oh fuck, oh fuck!' I leaned down to her chest; there was no movement. I put my cheek to her mouth: nothing. 'Fuckfuckfuck!' I lifted her down to the ground and shook my head, trying to rattle up a memory of CPR. I pumped her chest a few times, and tried to breathe into her mouth, but I couldn't seem to get any air in there. I adjusted my grip and tilted her head back, but still it seemed blocked. I rolled her to her side to try clearing her airway when I heard footsteps. I froze.

'She's dead, I'm afraid.' I knew that voice, and spun around. Dragomir. I was pretty certain he was smiling. 'You won't get any air in there; you've crushed her windpipe, you brute.' He lifted a cane to my shoulder, and used it to nudge me away from Ruby. I stumbled and fell against the pallets. He pointed the cane at me and I stayed there. From his pocket, he pulled out a tiny knife, like a mini Swiss Army. He knelt down, leaned in and sliced her neck, downwards from her chin. I wanted to do something, anything, but I was petrified. Blood oozed from the cut. He turned to me, winked, whispered 'bon appetit' and bent down to her neck. I thought he was going to bite her, or at least suck the wound, but instead he just licked it. After five long, deliberate licks, he sighed, stood and turned to me.

'Get out of here. Go to Ellison. I'll take care of this.'

'Really? Shouldn't I tell, like, the cops or something? I mean, I just killed someone...' I looked at my hands in the moonlight.

'And tell them what? You would end up in jail, and how long until they notice you aren't eating, or ageing? Just go, and do not look back.'

I've gone over that moment a million times in my head, and a million times I've wished that I took another course of action. But I was terrified and probably in shock. Staring at poor Ruby, I stood up and dusted myself off. I couldn't think. I took one last look at Dragomir, at the glint of the moon in his eye, at the redness of his lips, and I bolted.

Chapter Nine

I must have been getting fitter, or becoming more
'efficient', because I sprinted all the way back to my
car and was hardly breathing heavy at all. It took only
moments for it to return to normal after I sat in the
car, comforted by the familiar musty odour. I closed
my eyes tight and tried to think if there was any
chance at all that I'd imagined that, but even after all
the weirdness lately, I knew it was true: I had killed a
hooker, with my bare hands. How could I have not
realised what was happening? It felt like when I snuck
up on the girl in the fish store, like my mind went on
pause but my body kept going. Wouldn't Ruby have
fought back? I looked at my wrists and sure enough,
they were all scratched up. Shit. I felt wetness on my
face and wondered where it came from before I
realised I was crying. Movement caught my eye; my
boss inside the pizza shop had noticed me sitting in
my car and was coming around the counter. I started
the car, ripped backwards and squealed out of the
parking lot before he could get to the door. I had to
wipe tears away to drive, something that I'd never
done before. The only image I could see in my head

was Ruby, all bulging tongue and lolling neck. I started to gag, whipped over to the shoulder, threw my door open and spewed out of it. It smelled like bourbon.

By the time I got back to Ellison's I was completely worn out, shattered. I didn't even get to knock on the door, she opened it as I reached for it. I knew she'd be angry, but this was something worse. Her face was actually red, her eyes looked bigger, and she breathed twice in the moment we were standing there: she was practically hyperventilating. She opened her mouth, but before she could yell, she saw my face. She really was perceptive, because she softened immediately, almost as if she had compassion. I just stood there, defeated and miserable. She grabbed me by my collar and pulled me inside.

'I'm sorry,' I muttered, stumbling while she led me to the couch, my regular interrogation spot. I sat, and she got me a glass of water. I wondered why the sudden change and how she knew I was so shaken, then I realised she was tuned in to my feelings. I didn't know if she had the details of my night, but she definitely knew something was very wrong. She pulled her chair closer, sat in it said nothing. She looked at me while I looked at the ground.

'What did you do?'

I started to cry again. She sighed, grabbed my chin and pulled my face up so we were eye-to-eye.

'Uly? What did you do?' Her voice was so calm and soft. It was obvious she was trying to be gentle with me. I'd never seen her like that, seen that side of her and it just made me cry more.

'It's so bad... so bad.'

'Yeah, I can tell. I'm getting images of...' she waved her hand in front of her like she was wafting the smell of soup, 'booze, violence, sex...' she froze, 'death... and...' she sprang to her feet. The chair skidded. 'Dragomir?!? What the fuck, Ulysses?'

'I told you it was bad!' I started to sob. I drew my knees up and hugged them. 'I wanna go home. I want this all to be a bad dream.'

She was just staring at me. Suddenly, my feet felt funny, numb. I jumped up, only to realise I had no plan but to yell at her. I wobbled in place on account of the numb feet and pointed at her. 'No! Don't! I can calm down myself! I can do it myself! Please! Please...'

She let go of me, righted her chair and sat. I paced the length of the couch, concentrating on my breathing. I would absolutely not be controlled if I didn't have to be. After only about thirty seconds, I was ready. I sat, took a deep breath and told her the whole lot.

Silence. Then: 'you choked her to death?!'

'Yes. With my bare hands.'

'That's not optimum...'

'Not optimum?!? Ya THINK?!?' I felt my emotions swelling again. I closed my eyes and continued in a softer voice: 'correct. It is indeed not optimum, but I myself would go so far as to say it's

133

pretty darn bad. Horrible even. Do you not agree that describing the fact that I killed a human being as "not optimum" is maybe an understatement?'

She completely ignored my sarcasm. 'Uly, they are our source of sustenance. Yes, we do try to peacefully coexist, but for us to exist at all, they need to die from time to time. Think of it as if you had run over a dog while delivering a pizza.'

'Yes, ok,' I rubbed my forehead, 'but, see, the thing is that I have never fucked a dog and accidentally choked it to death, so excuse me if I am a little bit put out by the whole thing! What the hell, Ellison?!? You told me I wouldn't get, like, strong and shit!'

'Was she a small woman?'

'What?!'

'Was she small, you know, in size?'

I shook my head, confused. 'I guess, what's your point?'

'You're an average size man. You wouldn't need to be super strong to kill a smallish woman by choking her.'

I flopped back on the couch. 'Oh what? So you're saying this had nothing to do with me being a vampire, that I'm just an accidental psycho sex predator?'

'Not at all. Your sex drive has increased, as has your appreciation for sensation. I'm guessing the sex was amazing, and you completely lost yourself in it?'

'Yes...'

'And she asked you to choke her?'

'Yes.' I saw her face in my mind, her mouth whispering the request.

'Then the problem lies in your ability, or lack thereof to control how much of yourself you give over to these experiences. The good news is: we can work on that.'

'What's the bad news?'

'Dragomir knows.'

'He knows it was an accident. I told him I wanted to go to the cops, but he said no.'

'Yeah, well, that makes sense. He is always looking for ways to have something over me.'

'Why you? I killed her.'

'You're my responsibility, remember? You shouldn't have even been out alone.'

'But... it was an accident...'

'It doesn't matter. Neither you or I have a licence to harvest. In human and vampire law you have committed a grave crime. And Dragomir knows.' She spat his name as if it was the one sour cherry in the bowl.

'Oh shit. Well, maybe I can have a talk to Manny...'

She actually laughed at that. 'Ulysses, Manny is nothing but a sex slave to Dragomir right now. He holds no sway whatsoever.'

'Then what's gunna happen?'

'I guess we'll find out.'

'Ah shit...' I looked at her, right in the eye. 'I'm really sorry, E.'

'Well, nothing we can do about it now. Do you at least agree that right now, it's not a good idea for you to go out without me?'

I looked at my hands. 'Yeah...'

She lifted my head and kissed me, really softly on the lips. I thought of sex, she read it and whispered 'no', stood up and went to look out of the window. 'Go and have a shower, please.'

I don't know how long I was in there. I got a bit lost in thought, about Ruby, Ellison, Dragomir, Manny... the whole shebang. I missed Tony. I missed that normalcy, that familiar acceptance of my general asshole-ness. I wanted to see him, but I was afraid that I'd be overcome with the need to tell him everything. I missed being able to have a wank in the shower, which made me realise that I just missed having some time purely to myself and nobody else. The doorbell rang. I grabbed for my towel, dropped it into the water, swore, picked it up and held it in front of my junk. Ellison was looking at me, head cocked and chuckling.

'Tell them to wait a second so I can get dressed!'

'No.'

'Oh What? Why?'

'Because you disobeyed me.'

'Can you at least get me a dry towel?'

'No.' She headed for the door. The doorbell rang again, twice. I tried to remember where the towels lived. The one I'd dropped was sopping, so I left it and began to scurry about looking for another. I couldn't see any cupboards anywhere.

Ellison peeked through the spy hole and sighed. 'And it begins...' She opened the door wide. Without a word from either of them, Dragomir drifted in. She gently shut the door behind him, and visibly stiffened. I saw her take what looked like a deep breath. 'Dragomir, what a pleasure. Won't you come in?'

Dragomir stared me in the eye, then allowed his to descend my body. I cupped my junk. 'Vous permettez à vos enfants à être nue, tout les temps?' He indicated to me.

'Dragomir, you know I don't speak French.'

He chuckled, winked at me and translated: 'you allow your children to be naked all the time?' I didn't react; the last thing I wanted was Ellison thinking that I would ever team up with this guy against her. I didn't trust him even before she told me he was always out to get her in trouble.

She ignored him and addressed me: 'In the drawer under the bed.'

'So this is your latest... mate?' Dragomir gestured with a limp hand in my general direction.

'That's none of your concern. What do you want, Dragomir?' I loved her ability to cut to the chase.

'Come come, Ellison, we're old friends! I can't just drop by and see how you are doing? Catch up?'

'We are not friends, and no, you can't. Cut the shit. What. Do. You. Want?'

He sighed, and swanned to the window. He stayed there, staring out. 'I presume by now you know what your boy did tonight?'

'Yes. He had an accident, as we all have.'

He nodded, still watching the street. 'Yes, yes, we all have, haven't we... but usually there is nobody else who knows...'

'My god, Dragomir, you have a flair for melodrama. I fucking know you busted him doing it, and if I had to hazard a guess, I'd say that by now there is no evidence that girl was ever there, and you have yourself a few litres of free blood. Am I right?'

'You know me too well...'

'Good, then it's all sorted. Thank you for saving the day. You have my eternal gratitude. Enjoy your spoils. Now, get out.'

He spun to face her and before I knew he'd done it, he'd whipped out a phone and was holding it in front of her face. I couldn't see it, but I could hear what was happening. It was the sound of me fucking a prostitute in an alley. Ellison snatched it off Dragomir and looked at it closely. She rewound it. She rewound it again. She turned to me.

'You said she asked you to choke her.'

'She did! I swear!'

She brought the phone to me, rewound it and played it again. I recognised the moment she asked me, as I leaned in closer to clarify what she'd said.

But the phone didn't pick it up; we must have been speaking too softly. For anyone watching this clip, it looked like I simply decided to kill her for my own pleasure. I felt sick. I rewound it and showed Ellison the part where she asked me.

'I swear to you, she asked me to do it. She did.'

Dragomir, suddenly there, gingerly plucked the phone from my hand. 'My dear boy, even if you are telling the truth, nobody will know. This footage simply shows a sexual predator killing for fun.'

I sat on the bed. 'I'm not a sexual predator.' Everything felt very much out of control.

Ellison stepped in between me and Dragomir. 'Just tell me, you pompous old fag.' I was surprised at her use of the slur and evidently so was he, because in a flash, he was mad.

'I did this little maggot a favour, Ellison, and by extension, you as well.' He jabbed his finger at her. 'I got rid of the body, but now I have blood to sell. I can't sell it, because it's illegal blood, and because I am not a vendor. That's where you come in...' he purred the last sentence and it chilled me to the core. I had a bizarre thought, that I hoped he never got me alone. Being raped by Ellison was one thing, but I had a feeling Dragomir would kill me.

'What the fuck?! Why don't you just keep the blood for yourself? Why do you need to sell it?'

'I have wants and needs, Ellison. I saved your boy from many different unsavoury outcomes. I deserve compensation. You are going to help me get that compensation, or I am taking this footage to some people who will be most displeased...'

She sighed. 'You're fucking deplorable.'

'I'm an opportunist.'

'Whatever. Get me the blood, but for now, get out.' She pointed to the door, and it swung open. Without wasting any time, he sashayed out, and Ellison slammed it shut. She didn't turn around, just stared at the door.

I didn't know what to say. I couldn't tell if she was mad at me, or him, or both. I decided to play it safe.

'I'm really sorry, Ellison. I truly am.'

She didn't react.

'It honestly was an accident...'

'It was no accident that he got you on film.'

'Whaddaya mean?'

She sat beside me on the bed. 'What are the odds that he was just strolling through that neighbourhood and came across you two?'

'Slim?'

'Yes, slim. Also, there is the chance that he influenced you to zone out...'

'What?'

'It's harder to control the mind of a vampire, but only really hard if they're old. You're so young that it wouldn't have been difficult... what with you being already distracted...'

I stood up, didn't know where to go and sat back down again. 'Are you telling me that maybe I didn't kill her? That maybe it was him?!'

She looked at me, one of those into-my-soul looks and she seemed beat. 'That is exactly what I am telling you. I think he was following you, I think he influenced you to kill that girl, and he got it all on film so that he could blackmail me, us.' She got up and began to pace. 'For all I know, he's doing this to more vampires. I told you he was a douche.'

'How much money can he make off this blood?'

She continued to pace. I'd never seen her move without an agenda. 'The thing about blood is that as I've told you, we don't need much to survive, the older we are. That doesn't mean that we wouldn't like more. The balance between us existing and us dominating is very delicate. We can't harvest too much so that we don't upset that balance. Blood is licensed and rationed. If we allowed wealthy vampires to buy ridiculous amounts, then there would not be enough to go around. Each of us is permitted to purchase as much as it is deemed we need, within reason, based on our age and social position. Leeches like Dragomir can make a mint on the black market, harvesting illegally and selling blood at a higher price to those who can afford it.'

'Why doesn't he sell it himself?'

'Why would he, when he can blackmail others to do the risk-taking? It's a huge penalty if a vampire is caught selling illegally. It could even mean death.' She gravitated to the window.

'Fuck...'

'Fuck is right. So now, that douche has footage of you committing a crime. If you go down for it, so do I. He can name his price for that blood and my-our choice is to either sell it illegally, or face the music for what you did.'

I stood up and approached her. 'Then let's face the music. It was an honest accident. I wanted to go to the cops anyway.'

She touched the glass, ran her finger through the fog made by my breath. 'They'll kill you, Uly.'

'What? Even if it was an accident?'

'Yes, even then, and I might remind you that it doesn't look like an accident in the footage. As far as the government are concerned, I should have been controlling you in this crucial time. Young vampires are notorious for not being able to control themselves... It would be my punishment. I'd still have to wait the appropriate time to create another and I would have to watch you die. More than likely, they'd make me kill you myself.'

'Wow. That sucks.'

'Uh-huh.'

'But what if we sell Ruby's blood, then he says it's not enough? What if he keeps blackmailing us?'

'I actually think that will be exactly what happens.'

'What?! Then why are we going along with it?'

She looked at me; the street lights threw a soft glow on her face and she looked genuinely sad. 'What choice do we have?'

I suddenly had a thought. 'Fuck. Manny...'

'What?'

'How d'you reckon he knew I was there?'

'What do you mean?'

'Well, you said it was no accident that he followed me and filmed me. How would he have known I was there?' I had no intention of waiting for an answer. 'I'll tell you how! Manny, that creep! I met up with him in the bar! He must've told Dragomir where he was going!'

'Doesn't really matter now...'

'Yes it does!' It was my turn to pace. 'If we don't let on that we know Manny led him to me, then we could recreate the situation again, but in reverse!'

'What? You're making no sense.'

'No, I'm making perfect sense! I tell Manny where I'll be, he'll tell Dragomir, Dragomir will follow me, and then I'll trap him into doing something bad while you're filming it! Give him a taste of his own medicine!'

She actually laughed. 'That's the dumbest shit I've ever heard, but I like your enthusiasm.'

'Oh what? It could work...'

She began to shed her clothes and I thought sex. She chuckled again.

'No. I'm having a shower. I feel filthy for having that slimy eel in here.' She turned on the water, then looked over her shoulder at me. 'I gave you the benefit of the doubt once, and you screwed us both. If you even so much as think of leaving, I will castrate you myself.'

'Yes Ma'am,' I muttered and flopped onto the bed.

Chapter Ten

So, there I was: a brand-new vampire with no reliable ability to do anything better than I could before, alienated from my friends, potentially in big trouble, and stuck living with a cruel-at-worst, bearable-at-best female rapist vampire. Needless to say, I was feeling a little melancholy.

Once Ellison was done with her shower, she remained naked but gave me the eye, the 'no sex' eye, so I just lay there on her bed waiting for her to tell me to get off it. She didn't. She picked up a book, settled onto the couch and completely ignored me. The more I lay there, the madder I got, thinking about Manny telling that pale blackmailing motherfucker that he was going to meet me. He lied to me, again. He was either really scared of Dragomir, or really, really loved it in the rear. I was livid. I had only just started to enjoy my new life. What if I hadn't killed her? What if it had been Dragomir's influence? I was branded a killer now, because of him (maybe)!

Without looking up from her book, Ellison spoke: 'Calm down.'

'What?'

'I can feel your energy from here. Take it easy.'

I jumped up, stormed over to her and snatched the book out of her hands. 'Fuck you! Don't tell me to calm down! Two weeks ago I was just a regular guy-'

'You were a loser.' She inspected her fingernails.

'I may have been a loser, but at least I wasn't a murderer!'

'You're more of a predator now.'

I hurled the book into the kitchen and stood still, fists balled at my sides, teeth clenched, huffing my breath through my nose. 'Everything is fucked up! Is this how I'm gunna live the rest of... forever?!? Just mooching around being your sex slave and a sometimes-murderer? I hate this!' I was shaking, and felt both nauseous and like I might cry.

She stood, put her hands on my shoulders and looked me in the eye. I tensed up, anticipating slack-face treatment.

'I'm not going to control you; I'm just trying to help you calm down.'

'What could possibly help me to calm down?!?' I tried to shake free of her, 'I'm stuck with this! There's no taking it back, Ellison!'

'You could die if you wish...' her facial expression did not change whatsoever.

'What? Now you're going to kill me? Great!' I thrashed about some more, but she really was quite strong; she had me pinned.

'I would not kill you. I am strictly forbidden from doing so. But, if you hate this life so much, then you could end yourself.'

'You'd like that, wouldn't you?!'

'Not particularly. I actually don't hate you as much as I thought I would. Sometimes you're even funny. But if you're miserable I will not stand in your way.'

I gave up on the struggle; she loosened her grip and steered me to the couch. I sat, feeling tired and numb. She left me and went to the kitchen. I heard her pick up her book, then open the fridge. Moments later, she was standing in front of me, holding out a glass of strawberry milk. It even had a straw in it.

'Thank you.' I took the glass and slurped heartily. It was not strawberry. If anything, it was coppery. I held it in my mouth, about to spit it out when I realised I actually liked it. Audibly, I swallowed. I took another drink, and another until I was frantically slurping and gurgling at the bottom of the glass. I held it out to her, slightly breathless and whispered 'Can I have more please?'

She knocked the glass out of my hands, and when it shattered I heard every single minute crack and splinter. She bent down in front of me, held my face in her hands for a moment, then kissed me. She'd never kissed me like that. I kissed her back and she let me. I slipped a hand around the back of her neck; she let me. She reached down to check if I was willing and able, but I had been since the moment I tasted that milk. She moved her mouth to my ear and I took the chance to kiss her neck. It was impossibly soft, smooth and cool. She whispered in my ear.

'Do you want to?'

'What?' I murmured.

'Do you want to fuck me?'

I stopped kissing, realising the significance of her question. I considered my options for less than a second before I replied, 'Yes, please.'

She stood and dragged me by my hand to the bed, where she lay down, pulling me beside her. She grabbed my face and made me lock eyes as she whispered, 'Do not fuck this up.'

I knew what she meant: I couldn't treat her like Vic or Ruby. To be honest, I wasn't sure that I could control myself, but I knew she was stronger than me, so I felt fairly safe. I was just about bursting to be on top and inside her, but I was gripped by the need to kiss her all over. She was just so beautiful in the filtered moonlight, perfect, flawless. Before I knew it, I found myself on top of her but we still weren't fucking, just kissing. I'd always felt foreplay was a waste of time, but I was totally lost in the moment, and I couldn't honestly say how long we did that. She reached down and guided me inside her; it was better than I ever thought sex could be. Her hand stayed there, touching herself and it drove me wild. I didn't want to ruin it, so I went slow for a while. She grabbed my butt cheeks and pulled me into her, hard and it was all I could do not to finish right in that moment. As it was, I lasted only a few more minutes before we both came together. I was dumbfounded. Firstly, I didn't know that could actually happen (I thought that was just Hollywood stuff), and secondly, I could not remember a time when I'd felt more happy, and less alone. I flopped down beside her and kissed her shoulder, which I think surprised her, because she looked at me and seemed a bit puzzled. She rolled onto her side, and lay her arm on my chest. I didn't say a word, cos I knew I'd fuck it up, so I just caressed her back with my other hand and I guess I fell asleep that way.

I woke up early again, and alone in the bed. I looked around for Ellison and found her on the rug in front of the couch. She'd moved her chair and was sitting lotus style with her eyes closed. I was faced with a conundrum. I was hungry, but I didn't know how much blood she'd put in that milk the night before, and I wasn't about to wake her to ask. I figured I could wait to eat, so I rolled over, grabbed my phone to take my daily trip to internet land. I had a message waiting: Tony.

'Please talk to me. You're my best mate. I'm sorry things have changed. We've gotten through worse.'

I felt pretty bad. I hadn't even had time to think of Tony, with everything else going on. My initial urge was to tell him, which made me mad cos I knew I couldn't, and that would mean lying to him for the first time ever. I didn't want to get in a mood like last night again; I was still on a bit of a high from that sex. I figured I'd deal with it later, once I'd had time to bounce it off Ellison. I didn't have to think hard to formulate a reply.

'I'm sorry about what I said. I'm not mad at you, been holed up with a chick I met that night. Phone broke etc. I'll call u later man :)'

That took care of that, but I was still hungry, and Ellison was still doing relaxation, or whatever.

'It's mindfulness, not relaxation. They're two very different things.'

Gah. Her mind was so fit. 'I'm sorry, I didn't mean to wake you.'

'I wasn't sleeping.' She raised and I was struck again by her beauty and grace. I wondered if it would ever not affect me. 'Come here, I'll show you how.'

'Show me how what?'

'Show you how I made you the drink.' She opened the fridge and stood in front of it, like a regular person wondering what to eat.

'Is it just me or are you getting better at reading my mind?'

'It's not just you. I've noticed it's easier since our connection has strengthened. Come here.'

I felt kind of weird being naked—especially since she had put on underpants and a big shirt—but I wandered over, very aware of my junk bobbing about down there. She took out milk and blood, placed them carefully on the counter and looked at me, eyebrow raised.

'I've never met a dude who's this uncomfortable with his nakedness...'

I instinctively cupped my genitalia again. 'I guess I'm just not used to it...'

'You may dress, if you like. I won't stop you if you're uncomfortable.'

'Why did you put clothes on?'

'Because I sit cross-legged and I didn't think it was a very ladylike pose for nakedness.'

'Fair call...' I let go of my junk and resolved to get comfortable with it.

'Ok, watch me. Blood goes in first. Remember the last time you tried to open a bag?' I nodded. 'You do it like this:' She placed the bag on the counter and carefully unscrewed the top of one of the spouts. Nothing came out. She aimed it into the glass, gave it a gentle squeeze and counted out three drops. 'Right now you only take a little bit. When you need more, you open both spouts, so that air can get in and it pours more freely.' I nodded again. I was shocked to find how strong the blood smelled. I felt my heart beat speed up, or maybe I was just instantly aware of it. She filled the glass with milk and stirred it with a spoon, like it was an iced chocolate. She handed it to me, forgetting the straw. I gulped it in three swallows. I felt the coolness of it as it made its way to my stomach and instantly wanted more. I asked her.

'No, you need to wait half an hour and see how you feel. Too much can still make you sick. Now go sit, we need to talk.'

That sounded bad, but I felt so good after drinking that I was completely compliant. I felt kind-of happy. She pulled her chair over once again. I thought to myself that it was weird she never wanted to sit beside me. Maybe it was a power thing. She cut right to the chase.

'Uly, things have changed. Now that you—we are on Dragomir's shit list, it's just not safe for you to be alone for a while.'

'How long's a while?'

'Well, that depends on you, and how fast you adapt to your new body. The faster you learn control, the sooner you can have your space.'

'Well, this sucks! What the fuck-'

She held up a hand to stop me in my tracks. 'Ulysses. This is bigger than your petulance. Both of us are at risk here. Need I remind you that regardless of whether you killed that girl or not, you disobeyed me and caused a fair bit of general havoc? Any of that had the potential to get us in deep shit. You know I can control you if I need to. I know you don't want me to, and believe it or not, I don't actually want to either, but I will if I have to.'

'I thought you didn't want me living here yet?'

'I don't but things have changed.'

'Well what about my job?'

'Things have changed.'

'Oh, what? So I have to quit? Or are you just planning on riding along with every pizza I deliver?'

She sighed and rubbed her forehead. 'I don't like this any more than you do. You need to quit, Uly.'

'Well, how am I gunna get money? You can't just support me!'

'Actually, I can; I'm supposed to.'

'I don't want you to!'

'Why not? I made you this way.'

'Because I'll feel like a mooch.'

'Then start learning a trade. We can begin today.'

I felt heavy and sad. 'What about my friends?'

'You can still see them, but it needs to be around me. You'll need to tell them that we are a couple and have moved in together.'

I sat there staring ahead at nothing, and thought about how quickly my life had ended. It was suddenly clear to me that there were two options: be a cry-baby about it and constantly be unhappy, or realise that it's something I can't change, and try to make the best of it. 'Ok.'

She tilted her head back and viewed me through slitted eyes. 'Ok what?'

'Ok I'll do what you say.'

'Just like that?'

'Just like that.'

'No petulant demands?'

'Don't push your luck.'

She chuckled. 'I know it sucks, I do. But I really think you have what it takes to be a good vampire... once you get past the shitty part you'll start to have more fun.'

'Yeah yeah...' I scratched the last pitiful remains of my pubes. 'Well then, I guess we better get started.'

She still seemed shocked, but rode with it. 'Well, ok. So, here are your options for work at this stage, since you don't have any marketable skills: you could become a vendor, like me, you could become a harvester or you could test for Government. Of course, you can always undertake study to actually get a trade if you like, that's just a little harder is all.'

'Well, hang on. I have skills! I can make people do shit, remember? '

She guffawed. 'Barely! You make people punch themselves! Don't go testing for Government anytime soon!'

'Hm. I have to admit you've got a point. Well, can we practice it?'

'It's not a matter of can we, we absolutely must. The more skills you have the better: for you and for me. Plenty of vampires can't do that; it's a very valuable skill to have. It's a pity you haven't shown any promise for telepathic perception, though you've become easier to read...'

'Yeah that's a bit shit. Can I please have another drink?'

'Yes, and then we begin vendor training. Get dressed, and not in something stupid.'

'Like it's my choice!'

So, as it turned out, vending was a little more complicated than I thought. There are two main parts: the receiving of the goods, and the selling (or distributing) of the goods. Receiving can either be someone bringing it to Ellison, or her collecting it from somewhere. Distributing is the same, though she prefers to take it to the buyer. When she stores the blood in the meantime, it needs to be catalogued and dated, with the grade and two dates: date harvested and date mixed (and bagged). Like soda in a shop fridge, the oldest stock needs to be moved first. This can sometimes be difficult if she has an abundance of one particular grade of blend.

Ellison explained that if she had too many people coming and going from her place, then people would become suspicious. If police came to the door, suspecting her of dealing drugs, she'd forever be on their radar. That made sense to me. She had regular clientele, who always bought decent amounts; it was like she was the middle man, and those who bought from her stepped on it and took a fee.

Our first task was to embark on a trip including both a pick-up and a delivery. It didn't seem too hard. She explained that we'd do the drop off first, so the new blood wouldn't run the risk of getting too warm. Easy. Then she grabbed out the book.

It was huge, comically huge. It looked like it should say Vampyr on it, be covered in dust and contain a treasure trove of folklore. I giggled. She looked at me, puzzled. I figured now was not the time for her Buffy education. She heaved it open, to the current page. There were a lot of columns, filled with a lot of numbers. I inwardly groaned, but acted like I knew what she was talking about. She went through it way too fast. Somehow, from all that jumble, she got who we were delivering to, how much and what grade. I nodded and threw in an 'uh-huh' here and there; I think I fooled her. She pulled out a cooler big enough for a family picnic. Reading from her gibberish list, she plucked the appropriate bags from the fridge and gingerly placed them inside. Then, from her freezer, she pulled a bag of ice and poured it in, covering the blood completely. I thought that was it, but she reached into a cupboard and pulled out a box.

'What's in that?'

'A fake cake.'

'A fake cake?'

'Yes, we are off to a morning tea.'

Clever. The cake went on top of the ice. She scribbled some stuff in a notepad, tucked it in her bra and told me to get the door.

Once in the elevator, she instructed me to go to the basement. I wondered why and then realised: she had a car. I don't know why I thought she didn't, maybe in my head at that time vampires just flew everywhere. I started to get excited, trying to guess what kind of car she had. My best hunch was a sports car, like maybe a Corvette, or a Porsche Boxster. She chuckled. We stopped behind a little dusty maroon thing with no badge on the back. I felt my mouth curl up in distaste. She laughed out loud.

'Uly, we can't just be driving Corvettes around! Not when we do things like sell blood or kill people for it! Really only Government can afford scrutiny like that.'

'Well, what even is this?'

'It's a Volkswagen Polo.' She gave it a little pat on the roof.

'Oh what? Volkswagen?'

She curled her lip up at me now. 'What's wrong with Volkswagen?'

'Ugh. Never mind. Let's just get in.'

'You're a dick.' She popped the boot and lifted the cooler in, like it was empty and made of fairy floss.

'I thought you weren't supposed to get stronger as a vampire?' I whispered the last word.

'Yes, that's what I said, unless you practice it.'

'You work out?'

'Yes, asshole. I'm the strongest fat chick you know, wanna test it?'

I held up my hands. 'Whoa whoa take it easy... and I'd call you curvy, not fat.'

'Get in the car.'

'Yes Ma'am.'

She drove, but that was no surprise. I thought she would drive like a nana, but she actually was pretty assertive. We drove to the leafy green suburbs and pulled over in front of a massive house; I whistled through my teeth.

'Who lives here?'

'Someone in Government.'

'Figures... so I guess I'll wait here?'

'Nope. Only one way to find out if you wanna do this for a job. Come on.' She pulled on a floppy hat and hurried out of the car, leaned back and added, 'Oh, and grab the cooler.'

I felt a little under dressed, but I did as I was told. I'd been to a house party in this area once. I'd gotten massively smashed on their booze, fallen through a staircase banister (splintering it to bits), pissed in a pot plant and was promptly ejected and told never to come back. Needless to say, I wasn't feeling very confident.

I lugged the cooler up the stairs to the front door, where Ellison awaited me. She wasn't even panting from her sprint. She rang the bell. Almost immediately the huge door swung inward, revealing a tiny man in a tuxedo. I couldn't hide the look of shock on my face. I had thought that government men would be a bit more... forbidding? I mean, he couldn't possibly be that strong physically, he was literally the size of a jockey. Seriously, if you saw him from behind, you'd think it was a kid. I figured he must have wickedly developed other senses and stuff. I stiffened, thinking that he may have been reading my mind at that very moment. Ellison broke my trance.

'Hello, Jonathon, what a pleasure; it has been too long.' She extended her hand to his, and they shook.

'Ellison.' He grandly waved her in. 'And you must be Ulysses.' He did not offer his hand. I asked Ellison how many people she'd told about me.

'None, actually. Jonathon is simply excellent at reading minds.' I felt his eyes boring into my back, and though I knew it was the worst thing I could do, I looked anyway. He was squinting at me with just one eye; I barely had time to register which one before I lifted my right foot and stomped on my left. Ooh, all those tiny bones screamed at me, but I didn't react. I just turned and followed Ellison through the cavernous space, trying to think of absolutely nothing.

It took two rooms for me to realise that Jonathon wasn't following us.

'He's their butler,' she offered over her shoulder, 'and the best mind reader I know.'

'A warning would have been nice.'

'Yes, but then I would have no fun ever.'

We arrived in a kitchen that was bigger than my whole apartment. The walls were lined with subway tiles, like, floor to ceiling. One wall featured the sign Bergen St; I recognised it from a freaky movie I saw once featuring Tim Robbins. It was exactly like in the movie. Ellison told me to put the cooler on a counter. I did, then without thinking, gravitated over to the sign. I'd always been fascinated with New York and the idea of the subway... all those tunnels on different levels... it was like another world down there. I ran my fingers over the cool tiles. They weren't new and I wondered if they were the actual tiles from that station. I tried to recall the name of the movie.

'Jacob's Ladder, and yes they are the original tiles. I had them shipped here when they re-did the station...'

I whipped around to face who I knew—from TV—to be our city's mayor.

Chapter Eleven

He seemed genuinely tickled by my open-mouthed surprise. He ran his hand over the tiles too, and continued speaking, though it appeared as if to them, not me.

'I saw the film when it first appeared in theatres; I was just so captivated; it was unlike anything I'd ever seen... I knew then and there that I must have a piece of it, and when I want something,' he looked at me, 'I get it.'

'Wow...' was all I could muster.

'Wow indeed. In my games room I have signs from both ninety-sixth street and Union Square, both original props from The Warriors.'

'As in, come out to play-ay?'

'That's the one! I see you're a cult film buff as well as a subway enthusiast! Ellison my dear, where did you find this fellow?'

'Certainly not where one would expect a film buff to be spending his time...' She raised the eyebrow.

He laughed so heartily that it would've seemed fake if I hadn't cringed at it on the TV so many times.

'Let's see what we have here!' He slapped the cooler, and handed Ellison a towel, which she spread on the bench. She then opened the cooler, took the cake out and placed it on the towel, presumably to catch the sweat; it appeared like there was never a hair out of place in that joint. She carefully pulled the bags on top of the ice and lined them up so their labels were visible. The mayor leaned past her and perused the selection.

'Your PA told us you wanted a larger order than usual this month, sir. I brought a variety so that you could have some choice.'

'Ah Ellison, that's why I use you,' he looked at me and waggled his finger, 'it's the initiative that she has. Good vendors are hard to find.' I nodded solemnly.

'I appreciate that, sir.'

He spoke while inspecting the bags one at a time. It was borderline obscene the way he handled them; he jiggled them gently in his hand like they were detached boobs. He watched how they flowed when he moved the bag. 'I'm having a dinner party on the weekend. There will be all manner of guests in attendance,' he winked at me. He was beginning to really creep me out. 'I have plenty of fine wines for the plebeians, so I need some red for our older friends...' He was being so over the top with the hints, I felt like I was in a shitty high school play. If Ellison was feeling the same, she didn't let on. She separated some bags from the others.

'Well sir, these five bags are a grade four blend of middle to older aged men. All were smokers, so the blood is relatively low in oxygen, making it a deeper red. It's probably your best bet for something to pass as wine with a little water added, I'd think. These,' she waved her hand, indicating the remaining seven bags, 'are a complete cross-section of my range in stock. These two are a grade six, a blend of active twenty-somethings, these two are a grade seven-point-five blend of late teens with early-to-mid twenties, these two are a hearty grade five blend of non-smoking men between forty and fifty-five, and this here,' she plucked one last bag out, cradled it and delicately unscrewed one cap as she held it under his nose, 'is a grade ten, unblended infant.'

My breath caught in my throat, and I coughed, loudly. They both stared at me: the Mayor in apparent confusion, Ellison in rage. The more I tried to control it, the more I coughed and spluttered. Every breath felt thick and wet. I held up a finger to excuse myself and exited the room. I stumbled through the place, retracing my steps to the front door. From a hallway, Jonathon appeared, scowling at me and immediately my right arm flew into my face. I tried to dodge it as I hacked, but then my left slapped me hard, poking my eye in the process. I started to run, the door in my sights. I felt him behind me, as strong as if he was perched on my shoulder. I just frantically ran, my footfalls thundering and echoing off the walls, gasping for air and slapping my own face repeatedly. I burst into the blinding sunlight and felt the fresh air wash over my body. I hadn't realised how dark it was in there, I'd kind-of forgotten it was daytime. I collapsed on the steps and tried to slow my breathing. The sun felt really hot, even though it was quite early, but I figured I could sit there for a bit. I thought about what had happened. I was angry that I was so easy for people to control. I wondered if there was a way for me to fight against that. It would suck being everybody's puppet bitch for eternity. I then suddenly remembered what had started my panicked run in the first place. I felt sick, I felt sick because of what she was selling in there, and I felt sick with fear cos I knew she was going to rip me a new asshole when she came out.

I had regained my ability to breathe, and was just starting to get a little too hot for comfort in the sun, when I heard a man approach. Looking back, I still can't pinpoint how I knew it was a man, because when I looked down the street, he was far enough away that his gender—to someone less observant— wasn't clear, in fact I doubt his footsteps would have been audible if I were still human. Maybe it was something in his cadence, maybe I could smell him. At any rate, he was in uniform and was strolling my way. I didn't know what to do. I was too embarrassed to show my face inside again, but I didn't really want to have a conversation with him, and I was stinking hot. I looked around, hoping for a convenient alcove, or an entrance to a side veranda, but there was nothing. By the time he reached me, I was very awkwardly and conspicuously lurking on the front step; I sat. He looked up at me as he passed, and at first I thought I'd panicked for nothing. Then, he stopped, backtracked a few steps and crossed his arms.

'Can I help you?'

I leant back on my hands, as if relaxing in the sunshine. 'Pardon?'

'Do you need any help?'

'Um, no thank you, I'm just enjoying the sun...' I turned my face to it and turned it back; it felt like I'd been in a desert for days.

He leaned back and assessed me through hooded eyes. 'What I mean is, I know whose house this is, and you appear to be loitering. Are you bothering the mayor?'

'What? Not at all. I'm waiting for my friend who's visiting him.'

'Why are you not in there with them?'

'Uh, I wasn't feeling well and wanted some fresh air.'

He looked behind him, at the VW. 'This yours?' He jabbed his thumb backwards.

I slowly scratched the back of my neck, trying desperately to recall things I would be doing in his situation if I was relaxed and actually didn't have anything to hide.

'Huh-oh no that's my friend's.'

'Yeah well does your friend know it's in a permit zone?'

'Wha-oh... no, I don't think she does... I think she'll be out in a minute; they were just finishing coffee when I came out... I can get her if you want?' I yawned, though I didn't need to.

'What business does your friend have with the mayor, at this time of the morning?'

I put on my best shocked look. 'With all due respect, sir, I'm not sure that's a question you should ask... are you implying something?'

He clearly realised his mistake, and immediately held his palms out in a classic submissive move. 'Settle down, son. I'm not insinuating anything at all. Just making sure people aren't bothering the mayor.'

'Well, if you hang around a minute, you can see for yourself.'

Palms still out, 'No, no, it's fine. Just... tell him good morning.'

'Sure.' I looked back at the sky, giving him his cue to leave. He did, and I didn't look after him.

When I knew he was well gone, I gave up my 'relaxed pose' and started to frantically seek shade. I could feel myself burning. As if by magic, the front door opened, and I thought Jonathon had read my mind and was saving me, against his better judgement. Instead, it was Ellison, alone, with the cooler. She didn't even look at me, just stormed to the car and got in. I followed, and slid into the passenger seat, trying to think invisible. She put the key in the ignition, then turned to look at me.

'Do you have any idea how unprofessional that was?'

'Yes.'

'Do you know how much you embarrassed me?'

'Yes.'

She looked out the windscreen. 'What the hell, Ulysses? What even was that?'

'I don't know... I just... my breath caught funny... when you showed him the baby blood.' I scrutinised my lap.

She sighed and visibly relaxed. 'Uly, you know what we sell...'

'Yeah, but...' I looked up, over at her and we connected eyes, 'baby blood? Really? That's just evil.' I couldn't hold her gaze.

'Uly. Some babies die of natural causes.'

'Did that one?'

'Yes.'

I looked at her again, irritated. 'How can you possibly know that?'

'Because that's the only kind I buy, it's the only kind any vampire is allowed to harvest or sell. Nobody is permitted to harvest infants, except in times of dire overpopulation, which hasn't happened for decades.' She held my face and once more my gaze. 'I mean it. There are limits. But, just because we don't deliberately harvest it, doesn't mean it isn't rare, valuable and desirable.'

I looked out the window, up at the house. 'That guy's a douche.'

'Which one?'

'Yes.'

She chuckled, turned the key and drove.

I lost track of where we were going, just enjoying the drive. I remembered I hadn't told work I wasn't coming back. I text them my apologies, thanked them for everything, told them I was going to prison for a long time and that I wouldn't be able to be a pizza delivery guy anymore. I just couldn't be bothered with formalities anymore. Killing a person will really pull things into perspective. My mind wandered to last night, and I physically shook my head to chase away the visuals and tears. Ellison looked at me for second, but said nothing.

She drove into a back lane somewhere in Chinatown. There were chickens back there, actual live chickens in cages. Dust hung in the sunshine that filtered down and I felt like we'd gone back in time. She pulled up beside a door. I looked above it to a sign that read 'Ting Hao delivery ring bell' and looked for the bell but couldn't find it.

'C'mon.' Ellison popped the boot and jumped out; I followed suit. She grabbed the cooler and stood at the door. Her stance made it look like the cooler was full, and she was struggling under the weight. 'Ring the bell.'

'Uh...' I looked either side of the door frame.

'Up.'

I looked, and there was a string hanging down from the overhang, weighted by a single red bead. I pulled it, once.

'Delivery' she sing-songed. A slat opened in the door, eyes filled it for a moment, it slammed shut and the door opened. A small Asian man stood in the doorway. He nodded his head at me and grunted.

'Ciptaan saya,' she replied, whatever that meant. He seemed satisfied and took the heavy cooler. Ellison made no move.

'What did you say to him?'

'I told him you are my creation.'

'In what language?'

'Malay.'

'You speak Malay?'

'Clearly.'

He returned, with a clipboard for her to sign and some cash. I was confused; I thought we were only making one delivery, one pickup. On the clipboard was a list, written in (what I assumed was) Malay. She read it, and went down the list, ticking the odd item and writing a number beside it. He counted out some notes, handed them to her, took the clipboard and left. Ellison didn't speak to me, so I took the hint and stood there silently, feeling like an idiot. Momentarily, he returned with her cooler, carrying it like it was obviously empty. She took it with one hand, nodded to him, he nodded back and she turned around, put the cooler in the trunk and that was that.

Once back inside the car, out of the alley and the earshot of the chickens, I asked her what was going on.

'Nothing. We're finished for the day.'

'I thought we had to make a pick-up?'

'We just did.'

'Well, I'm confused. That seemed a lot like a delivery to me.'

She leaned over and hit a button. I thought she was turning on the air con. Instead, inside the windows rose another second set of windows, darker than the regular ones. I didn't try to hide my awe. She sat back.

'I'll explain. Try to keep up. Obviously, we can't just get around advertising that we are trading in blood: human blood, right?'

'Duh.'

So, when we went to see the mayor, it was under the guise of a morning tea.'

'Oh, about that-'

'Don't interrupt. That's what the cake was for. Then, we went to Ting's to collect my order. I need to make it look like a regular delivery. So, I present at the appropriate place for a food delivery, which would be in the back. I get out a cooler. I make it seem like it's heavy, because a delivery would be. He takes it from me like it's heavy. Inside that cooler is only ice and money. He takes the cooler away and brings back the menu, what blood he has at the time. I choose what I want and the quantity and he figures out my change right there. He takes the order back, fills it and returns with the cooler, which is full of my order. He pretends like it's light, I pretend like it's light and to anyone watching, I just dropped off a cooler of fresh fish or something, and got paid for it, job done.'

'Hm. That's actually pretty cool.'

'Think you can do it?'

'No.'

She glanced at me, 'what? Why?'

'Because I'm shit at acting, I get really nervous and besides, I have dyscalculia.'

'What?! What's that?'

'It's like dyslexia but for numbers and maths.'

She pulled the car to the shoulder. 'And you're telling me this now?!'

'Well...'

'Well what?'

'Well, you didn't ask.'

'I didn't ask?!' She lay her head on the steering wheel.

'I thought you knew! You said you'd been watching me for ages! How could you not know that?'

'So, let me get this straight. You can't do maths, and you can't act, which just happen to be the two main skills utilised in this trade. You have a hissy fit when anyone talks about baby blood, and you can be read and controlled by any vampire in a ten-mile radius.'

'Well, when you put it like that it sounds a bit shit...'

'It is shit! Why did I bother changing you? I can afford any sex toys I desire, so don't bother saying it's that!'

A thought struck me. 'Hey! I can't be that bad at acting! I fooled that cop that came past the mayors' place!'

She turned her head so slowly that I thought it might keep going, and spew green vomit. 'What.'

'That's what I was trying to tell you. When I was outside getting some air, a cop walked by...'

'And?!'

'I got rid of him!'

'You killed him?'

'No, I told him that I was waiting for a friend who was inside with the mayor having coffee.'

'Gah! What did he do?'

'Well... he kind of seemed a bit suspicious actually...'

'She looked to the ceiling and drew breath through her teeth. 'What. Did. He. Say.'

'I dunno! I can't remember!' I was suddenly very sweaty. 'He asked me what business you had with the mayor this time of morning! Or something like that!'

'What did you say?'

'I told him that his question was inappropriate and asked him what he was implying.'

She looked at me, disbelieving. 'You said that?'

'Yes, basically.'

'What did he do?'

'Panicked, told me not to worry about it and left. Then, I almost burned to death.'

She waved her hand at my flair for drama but added 'I'm actually pretty impressed; good job.'

I let a little smile out to play and mumbled, 'Thanks.'

She started the car and drove. I had a thought. 'Does the mayor have heaps of these parties?'

'No, that was a huge order and he bought it all.'

I cringed. 'What's the occasion?'

'I don't know, but if I had to guess, I'd say he's going to retire.'

'Why?'

'Because it's getting too dangerous for him to be in the sun. Can't be a mayor only in the night time.'

'Wow... what'll he do?'

'I imagine he'll take all his money to a big property somewhere that nobody will notice he's a real night owl.'

'Hm.'

'Hm indeed.'

I turned on the radio and found the Golden Oldies station. They were playing The Knack, My Sharona. It was right before the guitar solo. I held my breath waiting to see if they were playing the proper long version, or the weak sauce short one. It was the long one; bliss. The day wasn't a total loss, after all.

Chapter Twelve

I could tell that she had something to say to me, but I held up a finger and shook my head. She gave me the 'you better be kidding me' face, but I just pointed to the radio as the solo came on, closed my eyes and let rip on my air guitar. To my surprise, she waited. Once the song was done, I turned it down, and looked at her expectantly.

'Oh, you're ready for me to speak now, your highness?'

'C'monnn, it's the best guitar solo ever. Nobody should ever talk through that... man or vampire.'

'Uh-huh. Anyway, I remembered something I had to tell you.'

'What is it?'

'Well, though you don't give a shit where my blood comes from, I need to care, because I can be audited at any time.'

'Oh yeah? What does that involve?' My mind wandered to thinking about what happens when the cops pull her over for having really, really tinted windows. She reached over and pinched me, hard.

'Aargh! What'd you do that for?!' I frantically rubbed at my arm.

'Because you need to learn to have more control over your mind. I was speaking to you; it's rude to let your mind wander like that.'

'Sorry.' More rubbing.

'Anyway. What you haven't seen yet is the paperwork in the cooler, with the blood.'

'What's on it?'

'The serial numbers of every bag, which are traceable back to the harvester, and the source. It also has the info of how many bags total were in that order.'

'Waddaya mean?'

'Like, bag three of five for example.'

'Why?'

'Cos tonight, when Ting does his books, he'll go online and enter the amounts that I bought. When it's registered that five bags of five have been sold, anyone else that tries to sell blood under that serial number is screwed.'

'So, how do you keep track?' I was genuinely interested, but confused.

'I keep that ledger I showed you. When I bring stock in, I enter it. When I take stock out, I enter it. So, if an auditor comes to the house, I need to be able to show what I have in stock, that it corresponds to my ledger and receipt book.'

'What receipt book?'

'The one you would have seen me write in if you hadn't run out the door slapping yourself stupid.'

'...you saw that huh?'

'More like heard it. The slapping sound mixed with your coughing and grunting gave it away.'

'Fuck that guy.'

'Yeah, he's an asshole.'

'So, let me get this straight: if an auditor comes—which they can whenever they like—you need to be able to show that all the blood in your fridge got there cos you bought it legally off a harvester who harvested it with a licence?'

'Yes.'

'Is Ting a harvester?'

'Yes.'

'...Is he a ninja?'

'Don't be racist.'

'So, if an auditor comes and you have blood in your fridge that doesn't match your records, you're in trouble?'

'Now you're getting it.'

'Why can't you just put fake labels on it?'

'Some vendors do, but these days, with the technology we have, the auditors just have to whip out their iPad or whatever and check your blood against their list of what you should have. Also, from time to time they'll check ordinary vampire citizens, who have regular jobs and the only way they deal in blood is to buy it for themselves. If the blood they have in their fridge doesn't match their receipts, they can have it taken away.'

'Dang.'

'Dang is right. So now you see why it's fucked that Dragomir is trying to make us move this blood. If we get audited while it's in the fridge, bad news.'

'How do other crooks get away with it?'

'Oh, any number of ways... sometimes they're not registered vendors, so the auditors don't know to call on them. Sometimes they hide fridges. Sometimes, they even steal empty bags out of vampires' bins and re-use them, hoping they don't get checked.'

'That's beyond gross.'

'Indeed. To be honest, most of the low-lifes that sell illegally are linked to people that kill illegally, and people that buy illegally. I've spent a long time building a good clientele who trust me, and I do not want to screw that up.'

'Why go to all that trouble if there's so much risk of getting caught?'

'To make, or save money, exactly the same as when humans steal shit and sell it at pawn shops.'

'Is it that expensive?'

'Have a guess how much money I just took off the mayor.'

'I dunno, a couple hundred bucks?'

'Well, the five grade four bags were two hundred and fifty dollars each, the two grade six twenty somethings were three hundred each, the grade seven point five bags were three sixty-five each, the grade fives were two seventy-five and the infant? Well that was five hundred dollars.'

'That's a lot of money.'

'Oh, I forgot you don't math. That's three thousand, six hundred and thirty dollars right there.'

'Dang.'

'Now, that was a big order for sure, but there's a lot of money to be saved if he'd bought that under the table. The average vampire will only buy one bag a month, so the cost is quite manageable. But, the vampire who drinks to excess will go through anywhere from five to ten bags a month, more if they're loaded. And if they don't care to work and want things the easy way? Buy on the black market and get an order like we delivered today for a third of the price. Except for the infant. I don't think anyone's that ballsy.'

'Well what the fuck are we gunna do about Dragomir?'

'You tell me and we'll both know.'

We pulled up back at home about lunch time. I was hungry; Ellison offered to order in pizza. I didn't know whether I was evolving and getting sick of shitty food, or I was just over pizza, but I sure as shit didn't want it, in fact I was craving meat and veg, like a roast. She didn't even get out of the car, she just put it back in gear, backed out and started driving us somewhere else. I didn't bother to ask; I didn't need to. I was actually pretty content right in that moment, and the thought that she was going to feed me too was nice.

We pulled into a Red Rooster drive through and I could not have been more stoked. She ordered a full roast chicken with extra roast veg. The girl seemed sweet, and I felt bad for her that her till was going to be out at the end of the day, because Ellison slack-faced her, made her open the till, pretend to put money in it, close it and hand us a receipt. She let her go as the girl was handing the paper over, and the poor thing looked so confused. Ellison was nice as pie, thanked her and drove to the next window.

'So, you don't think you'd be a good vendor?'

I peered inside the window, wondering how long my food was going to take. 'Not really, no. What are my other options?'

'Pretty much a Harvester, or at least a Harvester's assistant to begin with.'

'What about Government?'

She turned, leant back and looked at me as if I'd suggested being a unicorn. 'You have to be pretty... slick to be in government, Uly. You're not really... sophisticated enough...'

'Couldn't I learn to be?'

'Maybe, but finding someone to take you on as an apprentice will be a struggle.'

'Dang... What about other trades?'

'How the hell are you gunna learn em? What's the average apprenticeship take? Four years? Trust me, by then you'll only be able to be in the sun for half an hour, max—especially since you were being such a baby about it this morning. You have a terribly low pain threshold by the way.'

'I can't believe after all this time, nobody's started a school for vampires...'

'What would we call that, Fang Hall? Blood University?'

'I appreciate the sarcasm. What about a night job, like in a service station?'

'Ugh.'

'What?'

'That's what the losers get: jobs like that. I'd rather kill you than let you bring that shame on me. You're going to have to try working with a Harvester I guess.'

'I don't know how I feel about all that killing...'

'Well, thus far, you're pretty good at it.' She reached out, took my food and smiled sweetly at the pimply teen working the drive thru.

'That was one time, and it was an accident!'

'Even better.'

'I don't really wanna be a killer...'

'That's how life works, I'm afraid. Someone has to do the killing, so that we can eat.'

I shifted the hot food on my lap. 'Well... can I just kill baddies, like a renegade or something?'

'I think you mean a vigilante and no; we've already had that discussion.'

'I'm pretty bummed about this, Ellison.'

She chuckled. 'I'm sure you are; it's not optimum for someone who's such a pussy... are you sure you don't want to give vending a shot?'

'All those numbers make me sweat just thinking about it.'

'Then it's settled. Once we're home you can eat your carcass and I'll make a call.'

She cranked the tunes and I think it's safe to say that we both tuned out for the ride home. Looking back, I think she was pretty worried about Dragomir, and probably trying to figure out what to do. I, on the other hand was just thinking how good the food smelled and wondering if Ting was a ninja or not, as she hadn't answered that question.

My carcass was delicious. I ate half the chicken and a good handful of potato but all of a sudden I felt very full, and a bit sick. I put the rest in the fridge and noticed that at some point, Ellison had already loaded in the new blood. I felt like a nap, and I must have taken one, cos the next thing I knew, I was being poked awake. I was really thirsty, like almost desperately thirsty and it took me a second to get past that and realise that there was someone else in the room; a man. He was chatting to Ellison from the kitchen, where she went after waking me. They paid no attention to me, and I wondered why she'd woken me at all when she returned with pink milk, and him in tow.

'Ulysses, this is George. George, Ulysses.'

I stood to shake his hand, and when I looked him in the eyes, I realised one was green and the other brown. He wore a short beard. The side with the green eye was flecked with sandy coloured patches in with brown; there were no patches on the brown beard, brown eye side. Naturally, I wondered if his pubes looked like that, and then I wondered if he just read my mind. Evidently not, because he didn't retaliate, though he wasted no time holding my gaze, and looked to Ellison. She sat in her chair, and waved her hand towards the couch. I scooted over, and we sat.

'George is a harvester, and as a favour to me has agreed to take you on as an apprentice.' I nodded, unsure of what I should say. George solved that problem.

'You're a bit scrawny, but we can work on that. Are you any good at mind manipulation?'

I sat and looked at him, realising my mouth was open but doing nothing about it. His voice was such a surprise. It was at least a full octave higher than I thought it should be. Physically, he was everything I expected a harvester to look like; broad-shouldered and bulky, he calmly simmered in his own faint sweaty aroma and cracked his knuckles while awaiting my response.

'Uh, no... I'm pretty terrible at it but I'm getting better.'

'Hmph. You ever killed anyone?'

'One person, her name was Ruby. She was a hooker and it was an accident.'

He chuckled, actually laughed at that. 'No more names and no more accidents and we'll be ok.'

'Ok.' I slurped on my milk like a bored child and realised they were both silent and looking at me. 'What? Are we starting now?'

George reached over, plucked the straw from my glass and threw it on the ground. 'We start tomorrow; Elli will tell you where to go.' He got up and headed straight for the door.

'Ok. ...nice to meet you...'

'Uh-huh', he tossed over his shoulder on his way out. Ellison followed and they hugged at the doorway. Words were exchanged. I couldn't hear them, but it looked like Ellison was thanking him. I felt like a real loser, and vowed to be a great harvester's assistant.

Ellison closed the door and crossed to the bed without saying a word. She rummaged through the drawers and pulled out a pile of clothes.

'Come here, please.' I did. She didn't look at me until I reached her. 'Ulysses, I'm sorry that you have to do this. I know you aren't very keen on it, but especially with Dragomir putting us under the pump, I really need to make sure you're learning a trade.'

'It's ok. Maybe I'll surprise us all and be real good at it.'

'I highly doubt it, but I like that attitude. Now, pick out a pair of pants and a shirt for tomorrow.'

'Bit of a shitty thing to say, but ok.' I started to pick through the pile, and found that they were all actually decent clothes. 'Why did you make me wear those ugly piece of shit clothes the other day if you had these here?'

'Because I didn't like you.'

'Oh.' I picked a pair of plain-ish Levi Jeans and a black tee shirt with a picture of a blimp on it, under a full moon. There were no words or explanation, just a blimp in the light of the moon. I liked it. 'Ok I'm all set. Do I need any other... equipment?'

'No. George will set you up with whatever you'll need.'

'Like what?'

'I don't know. It depends on his preferred methods.'

'Well... what are your methods?'

'I very rarely harvest, Uly. I haven't for a hundred years or so.'

'What? Then where do all these clothes come from? You told me they belonged to a guy you killed!'

'I lied. I got them from an Op shop in the weeks before I took you.'

Those words hit home. She really had taken me, from everything. Granted, I had been living a pretty shitty life, but it wasn't my choice to leave it.

'Well, when you did harvest, how did you do it?'

'I don't remember.'

'Oh what? As if. Stop lying to me.'

She sat on her throne and sighed. 'Fine. I took over their minds and made them hold their breath until they suffocated.'

'Really?'

'Really.'

'That's... kind of nice... as far as murder goes.'

'Yeah well I don't see the point of unnecessary suffering, don't make a big deal of it.'

'You make me suffer all the time.'

'Yeah but I'm not killing you. Yet.'

I folded the clothes and put them on the edge of the bed. I looked at them sitting there, innocuously awaiting tomorrow morning when I'd shower, put them on and get to work killing people. I knew I wasn't ready for it, but I also knew that I had to get good at something, anything so that I wouldn't bring any more heat down on Ellison than I already had.

She was on her chair, staring into oblivion. It didn't look like she was meditating, but I left her alone nonetheless, and flopped onto the couch. I pulled out my phone and looked at Tony's messages. I wondered if I could slip out without her noticing. I snuck a peek at her, only to find her staring directly at me, with that one eyebrow mocking me like always.

'What do you want?'

'Waddaya mean?'

'I can tell you want to do something. What is it?'

I looked at my phone. 'I wanna see Tony.'

'So ask if he wants to come over.'

'What, like, now?'

'Sure. It's early enough. Tell him to bring a date if he wants.'

'...is he in danger if he comes here?'

She rolled her eyes. 'Ugh. It's like we just met, you dick. I'm in enough shit as it is, why would I want more blood on my hands? Plus, I just told you that I haven't killed for ages and I don't have a current licence anyway.'

'Are you gunna slack face him?'

'Only if I absolutely have to. Honestly Uly, you must think I'm a monster. I actually think we're in more danger of you fucking up and making him give himself a black eye.'

'Yeah. Fair call...' I got to work texting my oldest mate and actually had butterflies about it.

Within five minutes, I was well and truly nervous. He'd replied straight away and actually agreed to bring his woman over. I told Ellison that we would both be meeting her for the first time.

'Really? Did he just start going out with her?'

'No.'

'How long have they been together?'

'Long enough to be living together and have a fur baby.'

'Ew.'

'I know, right? It's sickening.'

'Why haven't you met her?'

I got up and headed to the window. 'I dunno...'

'Oh really? Cos I think I do. You're an asshole.'

'You're probably right...' I pinched my fingers together in front of the setting sun, as if I was plucking it off a vine.

'What, no argument? No petulance? You've changed.'

'What? Oh yeah. Fuck you.'

'What's wrong with you? Are you nervous or something?'

I turned and faced her, leaning my back against the cool glass. 'Actually... I think I am...'

'What about?'

'Well, I have lots of secrets now. What if I slip?'

'You won't. Remember I can still control you, and them if I need to.'

'All at once?' I was part horrified, part turned on.

'If I have to, yes. God, you really underestimate me. I wouldn't allow you to bring people here if I thought there was a chance they'd see what's in the fridge.'

'Hm. Good point. What will we eat? And how will you get away with not eating?'

'Jesus Uly, relax. It's not my first rodeo. I'm almost a thousand years old! Give me just a little bit of credit, will you? Now, come sit on the couch and relax please, you're starting to stress me out, or piss me off, or both.'

'Yeah, alright.' I sat, and thought about the last time I'd seen Tony. I'd been pretty rude; I knew the right thing to do would be to apologise. I didn't even know what his missus looked like.

Soon enough, there was a knock at the door. I looked at Ellison; she tilted her head so slightly towards the door, and I knew she was allowing me to greet them. I could feel my heart hammering in my chest as I approached the door. I smoothed my shirt and opened it.

There they were. Tony was grinning, with his arm around his girlfriend. I felt my face relax into a smile, and I was instantly glad he was there. Just seeing his face was like crawling into a familiar bed, or going home after a long holiday. I invited them in, and he hugged me. In a strictly brotherly way, it felt great. He introduced her as Lucy. She was very nervous, and almost the moment I realised that, I wondered how I realised it. I turned away from her to introduce them to Ellison, and while exchanging the pleasantries, tried to pin it down. I could, like, smell and taste the air around her, or something. It kind-of vibrated too, like her heartbeat was sending out ripples.

I noticed them both look around the apartment, and I figured they were wondering where the table was.

'I hope you don't mind, my table broke and I'm waiting for the new one to be delivered. I thought maybe we could have an informal take-away session on the couch?'

Hm. I hadn't even thought of that. She really was good. Naturally they agreed, and we all sat on the couch, except for Ellison, who of course sat in her throne.

We ordered in Chinese, and Ellison paid, even though Tony gallantly tried to insist on it. He was obviously as glad to see me as I was him, and I relaxed pretty quick. Lucy was nice, though pretty boring. She was pure vanilla: mousey blonde hair, brown eyes, clear skin, straight teeth etc. There was nothing about her that stood out, but Tony seemed real keen on her and, looking back, I felt good to be meeting her finally. I never knew that it had kind-of hurt, being kept out as that ratty, not-to-be-trusted friend.

Exactly as Ellison had predicted, the night went smoothly, and after about an hour I was able to chill out and enjoy the night. Tony did look at me pretty weird when I ordered a vegetarian dish; I just couldn't seem to stomach meat anymore. I let him assume that it was something to do with Ellison, like I was pussy-whipped or something. It was preferable to the truth. She did have to slack-face them a few times: every time she took a mouthful of food she tuned them out while she spat it into a napkin. It was all pretty simple, really. By the time we were showing them out, I had renewed faith in my life being ok after all, even when I remembered what awaited me the next morning.

Chapter Thirteen

She woke me up at dawn. Ordinarily, I would have been ropable, if even wake-able, but surprisingly, I had no trouble getting up. I jumped in the shower and got dressed pretending that I was going to a regular job. It was just one surprise after another when I pulled on my shoes and looked up to see Ellison standing there with pink milk and a plate of leftover Chinese food.

'Don't get used to it.' She placed them on the couch beside me, then set herself up for some yoga without another word. I was satisfied to eat in silence anyway, so I munched away on MSG and watched her move. To this day, I don't know whether she did yoga to relax, focus or stretch; I never asked her. I figured at her age, she didn't need a lot of help with any of those things, so I thought maybe she just liked the ritual and I never brought it up. I guess maybe half an hour passed, I was finished eating and just zoned out watching her smooth movements when all of a sudden she stood, stretched towards the sun and said, 'time to go'.

Before we left the apartment, she gave me a twenty-dollar bill. I groaned.

'What? You have to eat.'

'I just hate being a mooch. I feel like a little kid; it's fucked.'

'Well, yeah it is kind of fucked, but that's why you're going to work. Now, get out the door.'

We made no conversation as she drove. I was pretty miserable, and completely unsure of what to expect. She drove out of town, and eventually pulled into a long driveway lined with huge trees. Their trunks were impossibly thick; I was reminded of a book from my youth and imagined people living inside them. The early morning light filtered through the canopy, covering the road in sun confetti. I felt like I was being shipped off to a stable to learn to play polo, not dropped off to my daily grind of murdering innocent people. The driveway opened into a clearing, in the middle of which was the biggest home I'd ever seen. I felt like it was one step away from a castle. Climbing the stone walls were endless vines and creepers. Windows were recessed and dark, and a mystery plume of smoke rose from somewhere in the back. A black and white sign informed us in an elegant script that we had arrived at Lockingston Canine Breeders.

'A puppy mill?!' I was instantly pissed off. 'Not only do I have to kill people you've got me working at a fucking puppy mill?!' Honestly, it probably could have been an organic, GMO-free, vegan approved cauliflower farm and I would have cracked it. I was really just looking for more things to rant about, and—though not a lot of people know this—I do hate animal exploitation.

'It's not a puppy mill, you berk. It's a cover. He has a few of his own dogs, and when they breed, they breed. Other than that there aren't any puppies. Relax, Doctor Dolittle.'

I still sulked. She pulled up in front of the house and kept the engine running.

'You're not coming in?'

'Well, I wasn't planning on it, but if you would like me to hold your hand and wipe your behind I can do that too?'

'Ugh.' I got out of the car, held the door and looked in. '...will you be back to get me?'

'I'll be here at 5.' She reached over, yanked the door closed and wasted no time leaving. I coughed in the dust, waving my hand in front of my face like a seventeenth-century lady. I felt ridiculous and childish. Once the dust settled, I took a deep breath, smoothed down my shirt and turned around the face the front door. It was already open and framing George, who was plainly scowling at me.

'Hope I didn't sign up some kind of sissy.'

I strode to the door, thrust out my hand and grunted, 'Morning, thanks for having me.'

He shook it—looking no less sceptical—and stepped aside for me.

His place was—surprisingly—not musky and dank. Thanks to countless down lights, the place was actually quite bright and inviting. The foyer stretched to the third floor, where they shared a ceiling. The staircase was grandiose: exactly what you'd expect to find in a vampire's manor. George ambled off and I supposed that I was to follow. He really looked a lot more like he was the caretaker of the place, rather than the man of the house.

I couldn't help my rubber-necking; the place was just huge. All of the inside walls were still stone, and I wondered how he kept the place warm in winter. Then, I wondered why I always think of stupid questions like that. He led me into the kitchen, which was tiled, floor to ceiling (and it was a high ceiling) in white.

'What is it with vampires and tiles,' I whispered. He didn't even turn around. It looked like a morgue in there and I wondered if it doubled as such. At the other end of the kitchen were two doors: one leading outside and the other (I found out after he opened it) leading to a stairwell that went down. Crisp, cool air flowed from it and I shivered. He shuffled through, and muttered to shut the door. I did, and had to wait a moment for my eyes to adjust. A glow came from below and I followed it; George was already gone. A full turn of the spiral staircase revealed that it was a flame torch, mounted on the wall. Inwardly, I groaned: how cliché. I could smell that it was gas powered and I wasn't sure if that made it more or less lame. It was muted in there; I felt like my ears were blocked or I was in a dream, or something. I crawled my hand along the wall for steadiness as I made my way down and naturally, it was cold and slightly damp.

I passed three more lamps before the light grew, and then I was inside another white tiled room, except this one clearly was a morgue, of sorts anyway. My senses were bombarded. Every footstep bore a dancing echo, fading as it fled. Light seemed to glow from the walls themselves and I shielded my eyes. Then there was the smell. It wasn't exactly repugnant, and I imagined that was because this room never really held any bodies in advanced stages of decay. It was just... sharp.

George stood behind a table on which lay a naked dead man. 'Whenever you're ready, Ma'am...'

I quickened my pace. The cadaver loomed. I saw his poor little flaccid penis and felt a deep sorrow for the guy.

'You wanna give him a little kiss?'

'No, thank you.'

'Touch him.'

'What?'

'Touch him.'

'Why?'

'Because you're going to have to at some point. Might as well get it over with. Touch the goddamn body.'

I carefully poked it in the stomach.

'Grab his arm.'

'Uhh...'

He gave me a look; there was no mistaking it. I was on thin ice. Slowly, I reached out and curled my fingers around his forearm. It was warm and I snatched my hand back. George chuckled.

'Lesson one: when we harvest, we need them to be as fresh as possible. I terminated this guy while I heard you pull up outside.'

'Oh what?'

'Yup. We only have an hour, max before the blood is unusable. So, we need to get to work. Go wash your hands and glove up.' He pointed to a sink behind me.

I staggered over in a daze, and did as he asked. I had no idea how he was going to drain the blood. I hated my life at that point. All I wanted to do was run out of there, up those creepy stone stairs and into the sunlight, while I still could. But, I knew that wasn't going to happen, so I took a deep breath, and returned to the table.

George had pulled up a small trolley with a bunch of silver utensils on it, and some new, empty blood bags. He held a huge syringe in one hand, and impatiently waved me closer with the other.

'Watch closely. I don't wanna have to tell you shit twice. I'm gunna find this artery for you.' He slid the needle into the skin, and I gagged. He shook his head but said nothing. Then, he rounded the table, picked a scalpel off the trolley, leaned close to the man's neck, gently felt it and then cut a tiny slit. I expected blood to spurt out, and then remembered his heart wasn't beating. It just kind-of oozed. George reached to the trolley again, and slid a tube into the wound. To the other end of the tube he attached a blood bag, which began to fill. I watched in silence as he waited for it to get plump, then he cinched it, took it off, attached another and thus it went for the next three bags. By the fourth bag, the flow had slowed to a crawl. George looked up at me.

'Now. Carefully, I want you to slowly inject that syringe without moving it from where I inserted it.'

'Uh...'

'Seriously. I don't have time to fuck around. Do it.' He stared evenly at me.

I took the body of the syringe in the fingers of one hand, and plunged with the other. I didn't dare look up to see if it was working, in case I slipped out of the blood vessel, but from the corner of my eye I could see him pull the bag off and attach another.

'Now, look beside you on the table. I put more syringes. You don't need to pull the needle out, just the plastic body of the syringe. Carefully remove it and insert another, and keep that going until you're all out.'

Without a word, I did what he said, until the last syringe; all in all, there were twelve. He tied up the last bag, and I counted six: three litres of blood. I watched him grab a little tube off the trolley and squeeze something onto the tip of his finger. He watched the end of the drainage tube ooze slower and slower, then eventually pulled it out and touched his finger to the cut, smearing whatever it was over the wound. He then rounded the table to me, holding up the tube. I held out my finger and he squeezed some clear goo on it.

'Take some gauze. When you pull the needle out, it will drip a bit. Hold the gauze on it for thirty seconds, then remove it and put the glue on. I'm gunna get this blood on ice.' He left me in the room with a dead body, but I tried not to think about it, and did what he told me. Once the tiny hole was glued, I worked up the guts to look at the guy, like really look at his face. He didn't really seem dead... he was a bit pale, but other than that he just appeared... asleep.

'Waddaya think?'

I just about had a coronary, and jerked back so quick that I knocked all the syringes to the floor. George deftly sidestepped the commotion and slowly circled the table while studying the cadaver.

'I pride myself on my ability to kill quickly and cleanly. Just because we need blood, doesn't mean people need to suffer.' He leaned over to inspect my gluing job.

'How?' I was gathering the syringes so that I could avoid his gaze, though I didn't really know why. Overloaded, I guess.

'How what?'

'How do you kill them?'

'I don't use any one way; it depends on the subject.'

'Subject?'

'Would you prefer victim?'

'No.'

'Fine. Then shut up and follow me. Pay attention. I'm not gunna repeat myself.'

I was glad not to have to look at him. I think maybe I was on the brink of crying, if I had to be honest. He led me to the far end of the room, and around a petition that I hadn't seen, as it was white-tiled like the rest. It took me by surprise, and I peeked at my watch to see how much longer until my day was over. We found ourselves in another room. It wasn't as bright, because a bunch of stuff lined the walls. All down the left side were big rubber body bags; hanging limp and silent, they looked like a regiment of grim reapers waiting to be assigned their victims. The end wall featured a grid of drawer-fronts, like the morgues I'd seen in the movies, and lined up the centre of the room were four more autopsy tables. In the far right corner was an industrial fridge, and then mounted on the right wall, arranged meticulously, their spots outlined in pen were several different kinds of weapons and tools.

'Go on, have a look.' George shoved me in the back; I stumbled and my shoes shrieked on the tiles.

'Yeah alright. Jeez...' The wall of weaponry and tools was divided into those two sections, and there was nothing particularly alluring about the tools. They were actually exactly what I would have expected to see in a morgue: scalpels, clamps, syringes, needles and various saws and saw blades etc. The array of weapons was fascinating and terrifying at once. There were three pistols, and next to each was a silencer. I'd never been a gun enthusiast, so I didn't know what they were, but I did recognise that they weren't revolvers. Above them were two rifles, and each of those had a ridiculously huge scope. The guns made sense to me—well, in the scheme of killing things—but then things started to get weird. Two compound bows hung on the wall; one was what I'd consider to be regular-sized, and one was comically large. Below the bows was a fucking sword that looked to me like it came from the set of Kill Bill. Lined up to the right of the sword were ten throwing knives, and below them was a spike protruding from the wall holding (I counted) six goddamn ninja stars. Further along there were several regular knives (the stabby/slashy kind), including a machete, and below them what I assumed was a throwing tomahawk. Off to the edge was a quiver holding the arrows for the bows, in addition to about 5 or 6 spears. Hanging above the quiver were various lengths of rope. There were two sets of knuckle dusters, and—I am deadly serious here—a mace. I'd never seen one before, and I gingerly tested one of the points. The chain clinked softly.

'I gotta be honest; that one's pretty much just for looks. I hardly ever get to use it.'

'Oh...' was all I could muster. I turned to look at him, trying to decide which question to begin with.

'How'd you kill him?'

'The guy we just harvested?'

'Yeah.' I jutted my thumb over my shoulder back to the main room.

'Well, I lured him from his place of employment...'

'Slack-face method?'

'What?'

'Oh, you, like, controlled his mind?'

He furrowed his brow, but answered, 'Yep.'

'Then what?'

'I brought him here, kept him dormant until you arrived, then stopped his heart.'

I stared at him, expecting there to be more. 'Just like that?'

'Just like that.'

'...did he feel any pain?'

'Not at all.'

I looked back at the wall of death. 'Then, why all the weapons?'

'Because it's not always that easy.'

'Why?'

'Come here.' He stepped over to the morgue drawers. When he opened one, I cringed and he chuckled. It was a faux drawer, and by pulling the handle, he actually lowered the top of a little fold-out desk. From inside it, he pulled out a ledger not unlike Ellison's. As he leafed through it, I saw that each page had a piece of paper stapled to it. He came to the latest entry, laid the book on the tabletop and beckoned me closer.

'See? There's a formula.' He pointed to the paper stapled in the book. On it were details of the dead man: his name, address, marital status etc., and then work/home schedule. Under that was listed the manner in which he had to die, how much blood was to be harvested, and what was to happen to his body after.

I actually gasped. 'It's all planned?'

'Yep.'

'Why?'

'Didn't Ellison tell you all this?'

I stopped and thought. 'Actually, she did... it has to seem random, right?'

'Yes, and remember, this man was bred for this.'

I shuddered, and looked back at the paper. Sure enough, it had him down as a heart attack, instructed George to take no more than three litres of blood and detailed that the body was to be left dressed in the early hours of the morning behind a brothel.

'Oh, that's a bit fucked!'

'What is?'

'Well, it says here he has a wife, and when they find him, she's gunna have to face the fact that not only is he dead, but that he probably had a heart attack fucking a hooker!'

George was incredulous. 'What the fuck do you care? He's food.'

I paused. I guess I couldn't afford to care anymore. 'Hm. Good point, I guess.'

'You guess right. Now have a look through the book to familiarise yourself with how we do things.'

It was both cool, and incredibly disturbing. Some people were down as suicides, some as muggings, some as hunting accidents. Some instructed George to drain the body and cremate it, others had him crouching in an alley in a race against time to drain just a single litre. Some needed to be completely brutal, some could be a coronary arrest in their sleep. I saw one that required him to turn off someone's life support in a hospital and wondered how the hell he could have pulled that off. It got creepier. There were some orders that just called for George to sneak in, take some blood and sneak out, leaving the donor to live another day. I had to admit it, it was pretty well planned. I got really caught up in reading, and before I knew it, it was lunch. George called me from the main room, and I followed him back up the stairs past dead guy, who was now dressed in business attire and looking decidedly grey.

We sat in his kitchen and had our 'food'. He simply sipped at a wine glass filled with blood. I had a cheese sandwich on multigrain and a glass of pink milk, darker than Ellison was giving me.

'How's the grub?'

'Good, thanks. I like cheese...' I scrutinised the neat triangle. 'I'm gunna miss it... shame you can't make cheese from blood, like you can from milk...'

George was silent, so I looked at him to find he was open-mouthed staring at me, his nose wrinkled in disgust. 'You are one fucked up unit,' he said, drained his glass and added 'I'm going for some sun. Come with.'

Of course, I wondered why George wanted to 'get some sun'. I asked, and he explained that he wasn't looking forward to the day when he couldn't be in the light, as that limited his work hours. So, he was trying to stave off that day for as long as possible. He figured that if he got himself a daily dose, then he could condition himself to withstand it for longer.

I never really liked the sun, anyways, I was never a sunbather. I can't swim for shit and sand pisses me off, so I used to steer clear of the beach. Being hot always irritated me, just like being cold. So, I wasn't too keen on sitting in the stinking hot sun just getting burnt. George pretty quickly told me to shut up and focus my mind on something other than the heat, so all we did for an hour was sit there in burning silence. Needless to say, I was very relieved when he said time was up, and I all but leapt to my feet and ran inside. He strolled, and paused at the front door for one last little bask.

'You know, you'll miss it one day.'

'I doubt that.'

'Whatever you say... c'mon.'

He headed back to the makeshift morgue, taking his shirt off on the way. For a fleeting moment, I thought he was going to have his way with me. Thankfully, I was wrong, and once we were in the main room, he shed all his clothes, made his way to the corner and turned on the decontamination shower. He stepped in, and I couldn't help but stare. He was so burnt. I could almost hear the water hiss as it hit his skin. He turned to face me and I saw that he was completely hairless, too. Thankfully, his eyes were closed so he didn't bust me looking. I had no idea how long he was going to be, so I went back to checking out the weapons.

Half an hour later, he appeared, significantly less red. He picked two pistols off the wall, opened another drawer, pulled out two boxes of ammunition and told me to follow him. We went back up through the kitchen, across the house and into a separate cellar that was set up as an indoor range. That's when things got a little more fun. We spent the next few hours shooting, or, rather George teaching me how to handle a weapon. I was terrible at it, though I did enjoy it. Until he took a mannequin out there and made me shoot it. It was a fully clothed lady mannequin and I missed every shot. He laughed and told me that I'd get better.

Before I knew it, it was 5. We returned to the morgue, and he pulled out a little black bag. He took a huge hunting knife off the wall and slid it in its scabbard, which had been hanging from its handle. He popped off to a drawer, and came back with a little black belt. In it, he slid the ninja stars. I looked at him, incredulous.

'I'm going to kill someone tonight?'

He actually guffawed. 'I don't think so! I just want you to familiarise yourself with these. Ellison will set you up with somewhere to practice throwing the stars. They come in handy more than you'd think. And I want you to get a bag of potatoes and peel them with the knife. You need to get used to using it without cutting yourself.'

'Oh. Ok, I can do that... speaking of Ellison, she should be here by now...'

We went up top, and looked out the front door: no Ellison and it was now a quarter past. George seemed bothered. 'That's not like her... actually, I've got somewhere to be, so I can give you a lift. Wait here.'

He rounded the drive in a plain silver badge-less car, I think it was a Honda. I jumped in and we rode to Ellison's in silence, which was fine by me; I had a lot to ponder.

I thanked him, grabbed the bag and headed up the stairs.

I was so lost in thought and overwhelmed from the day that I didn't register the muffled sounds I heard from Ellison's apartment, until I was reaching for the doorknob.

She was fucking someone. They weren't her usual sex sounds, but I knew enough to recognise her. I paused, unsure of where to go from there. On one hand, I was pissed: I thought we had something starting, and as much as I had fucked other people (and, let's be honest had no intention of stopping), all of a sudden the thought of her fucking someone else made my blood boil. On the other hand, I knew that she would probably kick my ass if I interrupted her. Then, I remembered she was supposed to pick me up. She left me hanging on my first day, and what's more, she didn't even put a sock on the doorknob.

'Fuck it.' I burst through the door singing 'Honey, I'm home!'

It was Dragomir.

It was not consensual.

He had her bent over the couch, facing the door. Ellison's eyes met mine. She was gagged and sobbing. I looked at Dragomir. He was already staring at me, an evil grin stretched over his vile face. He didn't slow, in fact he fucked her harder, licking his lips as their bodies slapped together.

I didn't know I'd reached into the bag until I felt the cool smoothness of the star in my hand. Dragomir looked to the ceiling, obviously certain I'd do nothing. On remote control, I flicked the star at him, and it barely made a sound as it lodged in his throat.

Chapter Fourteen

I stood there—frozen with shock and then fear—for, realistically, maybe two seconds. Half of that time, he didn't even notice the star was in there. Then, he stopped fucking Ellison and slowly reached for his throat. In that instant, I knew that I'd have to act fast. To this day, I don't understand how I could have been so incredibly bad at everything, yet in that moment do everything I needed to do. Somehow though, I grasped the fact that I had to capitalise on his assuredness that I was a plebe, and keep attacking until he was dead, or I would be, and very soon.

I grabbed the belt out of the bag and one by one whipped those stars at him as fast as I could. One missed, two lodged in his chest, one cleaved his cheek open, and one grazed Ellison's behind before slicing into his lower abdomen. He let out a shrill scream and pushed off Ellison, reeling back as if she were the source of the sudden pain. I dropped to the ground, slid the knife out of the bag and its sheath and crawled towards him as fast as I could. I slashed at his heel, maybe thinking that I'd cut his Achilles and he'd fall, or something. The knife was way sharper than I'd anticipated; it slid into his flesh so easily, and hit bone. I gagged.

Dragomir let out a roar this time, and looked down at me. I'll never forget the look in his eyes. I imagine it's infuriating for anybody to be bested by someone inferior at fighting and things of that nature, but I reckon it's a million times worse when that person is wickedly old, strong and supposedly immortal. He seemed so mad that even he was confused. He just screamed at me, his eyes bulging out of his head, his face split wide open. I could see his tongue pulsing while he raged.

Blood gushed, I gagged, Dragomir stumbled and reached for me. I scrambled to get away, but slipped in his blood and fell flat on my face in it. Then I was properly retching. The knife skidded away; I tried to crawl after it but he had my leg. I kicked, and my shoe came off in his hands. Before I could move, he had me around the ankle again, but the blood must have tripped him up too, because his grip slipped and he found himself with the bottom of my pants leg. I lunged forward, grabbed at my waistband and helped it down a little. Dragomir did the rest by continuing to pull. When my leg was out, I flipped onto my bum, kicked my shoe off and frantically shoved the other leg down and off, into his face. I used that second to spin around, grab the knife and turn around just as he was about to pounce on me.

I remember being incredulous about the fact that he leapt right onto the blade. It sunk into the base of his neck, and I felt it pop through a few tougher things in there. The thing that made me feel sickest of all in hindsight was the fact that in that tiny moment, I felt a rush of pure joy.

He made the most awful, guttural gurgling. I didn't stop. He was a vampire for fuck's sake. I twisted the knife, and tried to jerk it around as best I could. It pretty much completely sliced open one side of his neck. His head began to bob at a funny angle, and that's when I got the idea. Nobody, immortal or not can survive beheading.

I jerked the knife back out and scooted away a bit. He was definitely weaker, but no less angry. He clawed at air in my direction. I grabbed him by his hair, hoping to flip him over, sort-of by his head. Instead, I just turned his head around at a sickeningly unnatural angle. I baulked but didn't gag for once; I think I was past that. All of a sudden, he went quiet, and all I could hear was my own breathing.

He looked me right in the eyes and in a raspy whisper, hissed, 'Please... I'm sorry'.

I wish I'd thought of a witty line, or even a poignant one. But I didn't. All I could think of was the image of him raping her. I stood up and pulled his head with me. It tugged at his ruined throat, and I heard things break. It was only holding on by his spine and half the connective tissue. Aiming the knife away from me, I held it against his neck and gave myself a moment to turn back.

'Fuck it.' I whispered, and slashed as hard as I could.

The soft tissue was no problem, and then I was mostly just hacking at neck bones. Thankfully, it only took a few good, hard whacks and his body slumped to the floor. It sounded so wet. I just stood there. His head slipped out of my hand, followed by a muted thud. I heard a clatter, and realised I'd dropped the knife, too.

I looked up, and there was Ellison. She must have pulled her pants up, but now her arms hung at her sides like pale, dangling eels. Her face showed no emotion, in fact the only hint that she'd been crying was her wet cheeks. She just stood there.

'Say something.' My voice was hoarse, and I wondered if maybe I'd been screaming too.

'You killed him.'

'Yeah, I'm pretty sure...' I nudged the severed head with my foot; it was so... slack. The tongue lolled out a bit and I thought of poor Ruby. 'Why does everyone keep dying during sex?'

'Well, because you keep killing them.'

'Am I in trouble?'

'With who?'

'You?'

She cocked her head the tiniest bit, then, slowly, walked towards me. As she passed Dragomir's body, she kicked it—hard—to make room for her to get to me. She stood right in front of me, and for a second I thought she was going to maybe kiss me, which would have been weird. Instead, she wrapped her arms around me, laid her head into my neck and squeezed.

'You're certainly not in trouble with me. Thank you.' She pulled back to take me in. 'Am I surprised?

Yes. You seemed like such a pussy around the idea of harvesting, I didn't think you had something like... this...' she gesticulated my mess, 'in you.'

'To be honest, I didn't think about it. I didn't, like, plan to kill him, I just kind-of saw red, when I came in and he was...'

She didn't break our gaze. 'Raping me, you can say it.'

'How the hell... like, why...'

'How'd it happen, you mean?'

'Yeah, and are you ok?' I was starting to calm down and have proper thoughts again.

'I'll tell you when we've cleaned up. And, also, you're hurt.' She pulled up my shirt, and sure enough, blood was oozing from two different cuts, one on my lower abdomen, one just under my ribs.

'What the...?'

'When he lunged at you before you stuck the knife in his throat, the stars you stuck in him must've cut you too. Sit.' She pointed to the couch. 'Actually, you're covered in blood...' she grabbed a towel, put it down and I sat. She fished around in the kitchen cabinets. 'I can't believe George gave you those stars, actually! What was he thinking? And that knife? Why not just a sword?'

'He has one, you know.'

'Not even surprised...' She returned, juggling a bunch of first aid supplies. I sat very still and watched her work. She poured Hydrogen Peroxide on the cuts; it gently fizzed. 'These aren't too bad... I don't know whether to stitch them or not...' She carefully prodded around.

'Stitch them? With what?'

'A needle, duh. Anyways, I don't think you need it. I reckon you'll be a bit better at healing by now, and as long as we're careful, I think you can get by with some butterfly strips...' She pulled out the box, and dressed the cuts. Neither of us spoke for a while.

'I really killed him...'

'Yeah, you really did.'

'Why didn't we just do that earlier, when he was blackmailing us?'

She looked at me with that raised eyebrow. 'Because it's illegal.'

'It's just as illegal now.'

'Yes but this was a crime of passion...' trailing off, she sat back, staring at me. 'Speaking of that, what a funny turn of events, don't you think?'

'How so?'

'I've raped you before.'

I looked down. 'I know.'

'I've been horrible to you.'

'I know.'

'I've made you angry, several times.'

'Yeah.'

'I bet you've wanted to kill me.'

'Maybe.' I looked up. 'I wouldn't have, though.'

'Because you know you don't stand a chance in hell?'

'No, because I like you, kind-of.'

'Uly, do you know why I raped you those times, and treated you like shit?' She went back to dressing.

'I never really thought about it.'

'Think now.'

'Well, I guess you needed to show me who's boss?'

'Hm. Sort-of. I've lived through years of a patriarchal society, like, hundreds of years.' She held up two packs of band-aids. 'Fabric or plastic?'

'Plastic, I'm allergic to fabric.'

'Not for long. Anyway, I guess a part of me takes payback in that way. For as long as we've been here, people and vampires, men have been raping women. They're generally stronger, and hide behind things like "having needs" and "she said no but she meant yes", etc, etc.'

'Ok.'

'Within the last hundred years or so, women have begun to fight back, in lots of ways, for equal social status, equal pay, stuff like that.'

'You mean feminism?'

'Oh, you've heard of it?' She winked at me. 'Yes, feminism. The biggest part of that is claiming an equal stance. I guess me forcing us to have sex while I have the ability to was my way of asserting myself, so you would know I'm never less than you...'

'Still kind of fucked, though. Rape is rape. You made me cry.'

'Yep, you're totally right. And, after tonight, no more rape, you have my word. But, you do need to remember that I'm still in charge, because I'm still responsible for you, at least for the next hundred years. If you play the game, we'll be fine. If not, I will punish you, but it will no longer be sexual in nature.'

'Ok.'

She laughed, 'ok? That's all you have to say about all that?'

'I forgive you for raping me.'

'Well, thank you.' She finished with the band-aids and made herself comfortable beside me.

'So, what happened?'

She took a deep breath, pushed it out through pursed lips and began. 'It was about a quarter to five. I'd lost track of time and was rushing around to get out the door. As much as I make out I don't give a shit about you... well... anyway, I knew you'd probably be ready to go right at 5, so I was trying to hurry. I literally opened the door and there he was... grinning at me... fuck...' she shuddered. 'He pushed his way in. I told him that I didn't have time to talk and that he'd have to come back later. He got really mad...' she hugged herself, 'he started yelling at me and waving around a big bag he'd brought. It was full of packages of Ruby's blood.'

'You called her by her name...'

'Yeah well... as soon as Dragomir started using her, she became a little more than just a dead chick to me...' I took her hand and without raising her head, she continued. 'I was pretty mad too. I was pissed off that he'd barged in, pissed off that he was blackmailing us and pissed off that I was scared. I told him that I didn't care what he did, or who he told, that I wasn't going to sell his blood for him, and I told him to get out.'

'What did he do then?'

'He just sort-of... went silent, for a moment... staring at me. Then, he starting walking towards me. I was really scared, Uly, and I haven't felt that for a long, long time. I backed up, and we ended up on this side of the couch. I tried to backpedal, telling him that I'd sell whatever he wanted, but that I had to go, so please could he leave. He didn't say anything, just kept staring and getting closer to me. Then, before I knew what was happening, he had me bent over the couch. He ripped my underwear off, shoved them in my mouth and pinned my arms before I had a chance to even think about screaming. I tried to enter his mind, but he's too strong... was too strong... It was only about thirty seconds later that I heard you outside the door.'

She'd gone so quiet, and hung hear head. I lifted it, so I could look at her.

'Is this shame? Embarrassment?'

'I don't know... maybe?'

'Nope. I won't let you. No way are you going to give that filthy dead pig the satisfaction. None of that was your fault, none. Sometimes people are bigger than us, stronger than us and poisonous inside, and they do shit like that. You stood up for yourself, and he was evil, end of story. I'm glad I killed that cunt, I wish I'd had the time to torture him, too.'

She didn't break my gaze, and her eyes let loose tear after tear. 'Uly, I'm so sorry.'

I hugged her, and she let me, for the first time. It was so weird, cos it felt sort-of nice, and there was a severed head right by our feet. We just sat there for a while and let silence calm us down. After a second, she pulled away, and held me at arm's length.

'How did you do that?'

'What?'

She stood up and looked at the whole mess, her eyes huge and growing. She scanned it several times. 'Like, it just hit me. You killed a really, really old vampire. I mean, I'm very good at mind control, and I didn't have a hope in hell with Dragomir. He was in complete control of that situation...' she walked around the couch to the front door, 'I was utterly helpless and you, you came in and just, like, neutralised him, special ops style... I don't mean to be rude, but, how the fuck...'

She turned around. 'Did you know you could do that?'

'What, kill someone? I only did it once, accidentally, you know that.'

'Well, that's what you tell me.'

'What are you inferring?'

'You mean insinuating. What I am insinuating is that you've been keeping this from me, somehow, and you're playing me. Is all this aversion to harvesting a game to you?'

'What?'

She didn't answer, just stared at me, and I could feel her getting madder by the second. I held up my hands.

'Ellison. You've been watching me for ten years, you said so yourself. How in the hell could I have hidden something like this,' I waved my hand grandly over the horrid scene I'd created, 'how could I have kept that a goddamn secret?'

She still stared at me, but I made sense and she knew it. She looked around at all the blood, hands on her hips. She looked like a dishevelled Peter Pan. 'I just cannot believe you hit him in the throat with a shuriken.'

'A what?'

'A ninja star.'

'Yeah, he didn't even know at first... I did miss him with one... sorry.'

'More to the point, you got him with five!'

'I know, right? And that knife, whoa... and did you know George has, like, a whole arsenal in there?'

'No, but I can guess. Uly,' she looked up at me, 'what the fuck are we going to do with his body?'

'Chop it into little pieces and hide it places?'

'What? How is that the first place your mind goes?'

'Too much?'

'Way too much. We need this cleaned and disposed of before anybody can miss him though, or before anyone finds out.'

'You think Manny will be mad?'

'I neither know or care, that is at the bottom of my list of priorities right now. We need garbage bags and towels, for a start.'

'We could call George? He could bring a body bag around?'

'Ulysses, I can't stress this enough. What we have done here is a grievous crime. We could be put to death for this.'

'You didn't do anything, this is all me, and it was self-defence!'

'No, it wasn't. You were defending me, and you killed a vampire. Whatever the case, we could end up convicted and I'm not willing to take that chance. No, we can't tell George, we can't tell anyone.'

'Tell anyone what?' In the doorway, behind Ellison, looking cheery and chipper as usual was the Mayor. He peered around her. 'Oh. I guess you mean that.'

Chapter Fifteen

I hadn't even registered that the door was still open, as I'd left it when I charged in. Ellison whipped around, grabbed the mayor, pulled him inside by his collar and slammed the door. She immediately let him go and smoothed his front, but he appeared not to notice; he just kept trying to see around her.

'Wow... you made a real mess there.'

She held her forehead in her hand. 'In more ways than one, it seems. Hello, sir.'

'Hello my dear. May I come in?' he was already wandering over to the collected parts of Dragomir. And who is this?'

'It's a long story, I better get you a drink. Sit by Uly, sir.' She made her way to the kitchen and pulled a bag out of the fridge. I wondered if she was getting him baby blood. The mayor stood in front of me and for a moment I thought that I probably should have stood up to shake his hand or something. He looked at me with pity face and I realised I was in the clear. He sat.

'You poor boy, you've been injured...' he took me in further, 'you're covered in blood!'

'I'm ok, it's not all mine, and Ellison patched me up.' He didn't speak further, so I added, 'It's good to see you again, sir', and instantly regretted it.

Thankfully, Ellison appeared with the mayor's red, handed it to him and gave me pink milk. It had, all of a sudden, become quite a bit darker. She sat in her chair opposite us, without even glancing at the headless corpse that lay almost between us all, off to one side of the couch.

'That,' she nodded her head to the body, 'is Dragomir—was Dragomir.'

'Did I know him? I... can't see... the face.'

'I'm not sure, sir, but I dare say you would've remembered him. He was... memorable.'

'How did he come to be dead in your living room?'

She took a deep breath. 'Look, sir, I'm just going to tell you everything. I don't see the point of hiding anything, now that we're sharing a drink in the company of a headless vampire.'

'Very well.' He took a sip. 'Begin; I'm all ears.'

'Well, as you know, Uly—Ulysses is my creation. I created him according to the specifications of the law; there is nothing amiss there.'

'I would expect nothing less from you.'

She grimaced slightly. 'He's been progressing quite well; he shows promise in telekinesis and is keen to learn and contribute in any way he can... having said that...' she watched me wipe off my milk moustache, 'he has made... errors.'

Though I knew it was potentially a mistake, I butted in. 'It's not her fault, sir. I was an asshole. I left one night, went out on my own... she told me not to and I didn't listen. I messed everything up. I killed someone sir. It was an accident, but it happened.'

'Well yes, that's obvious.' He nodded to the corpse.

'Thank you, Ulysses for taking responsibility, but the blame is mine. Not this vampire, sir. He killed a human, a woman. This vampire saw the whole thing and was blackmailing us—to sell her blood—as a result.' She pointed to the bag sitting by the front door. 'The blood is in there.'

He looked at me, confused. 'How did he catch you?'

'Well, sir... I was having sex with her at the time, and I kind-of zoned out. Maybe he crept up, maybe he even controlled my mind to make me do it, I can't be sure. All I know is that when I realised she was dead, he was there.'

'Was there anybody with him?'

'No, sir.'

'What did he do?'

'He told me to run. I told him that I wanted to call the police but he told me they wouldn't believe me and that it'd be worse. I was scared... so I did what he said.'

'How did he come to be blackmailing you?' He looked back at Ellison.

'He knew Uly is mine. Him and I have a history; we were not friends. He came here and stated his terms. They were to sell the blood or he would inform the government of Uly's crime.'

'Do you think anyone else knew about this?'

'I can't be too sure, but if I know Dragomir, then I would say not. He was abrasive, pompous and nasty. I never knew him to have an entourage. I assume he worked alone, or maybe with his protégé.'

'So what you're saying is that it's likely that the only people who know that Ulysses killed a woman are in this room, with the possible exception of one other?'

'Yes, sir.'

'Have you met his protégé?'

'Actually, yes. And Uly already knew him.'

He stood up; he seemed more comfortable thinking on his feet. 'Then this isn't as bad as it could be. Is that why you killed this vampire?' He gave a quick wave towards the carnage.

'Uh, not as such.'

The mayor reached the window and placed his palm on it, looking down on the street below. He turned around and leaned against the glass. 'Mm. That's warm.' He closed his eyes and moved around, like an itchy bear against a tree. 'Then if it wasn't as simple as killing the vampire who was blackmailing you, what happened to produce the scene before me?'

Ellison filled him in, glossing over the rape as best as she could; it was obviously hard for her to speak about it. She got to the part where I busted in.

'I heard him outside the door and felt his hurt. He could tell something sexual was happening. I think he may have thought that I'd decided not to pick him up from work in lieu of some afternoon delight...'

The mayor interrupted: 'you have a job, Ulysses?'

'Sort-of. An apprenticeship I guess. I don't really like it but I don't have a choice.'

'Vending?'

'No sir, harvesting. I was bad at vending.'

He waved his hand at Ellison, 'Continue.'

'Anyway, he threw open the door and was faced with it, head-on. I felt his irritation turn to confusion and rage. He picked something out of his bag and flung it at Dragomir; I was surprised how quick he was. I didn't even get time to see what he threw.'

'What was it?'

'A shuriken.'

'A ninja star?'

'Yes!'

'Did it hit him?'

'Yes! It lodged in his throat! A goddamn shuriken! I don't even think Dragomir realised at first. Then, when he did, Ulysses flung five more at him, and only missed with one!'

'That's either brilliant or lucky...'

'Well, it could have been luck, but I don't think so, sir. Trust me, nobody was more shocked than me to see Uly do something like that.'

'Hey! I'm right here, you know!' I drained my milk.

'Well... you have to admit, you've not shown a lot of promise... physically...'

I grunted.

'Anyhow, then Dragomir staggered backwards, and I thought he was going to kill Uly, but—and this is why I don't think it was luck—Uly dropped to the floor, pulled out a giant bowie knife, crawled over and slit Dragomir's Achilles!'

'Really?'

'Really.'

He looked to me. 'Did you have training in this sort of thing in your human life?'

'No sir, I was a pizza delivery driver.'

'Seriously?'

'Uh, yes.'

He looked back to Ellison, 'what then?'

'There was a struggle. Uly managed to kick him off, but he regrouped quickly and pounced... right onto the knife. Uly was surprisingly ruthless. He twisted it and jerked it around; it was brutal.'

'Is this true?' He held his chin as he regarded me.

'Yes, sir.'

'Did you like it?'

'Pardon?'

'Did you like it? What did it feel like?'

'I... I don't know...'

'Be honest with me, please. You know I'll be able to tell if you're not.'

I stared at him. 'It felt good. I liked it. I kind-of hated myself for liking it, but I know it felt good.'

'Thank you. At what point did he fully decapitate him?' Back to addressing Ellison.

'Right after that. He stood up, holding Dragomir by the hair. Dragomir begged for his life, and then Ulysses hacked his head off.'

'Just like that?'

'Just like that.'

'Interesting.'

'I know, right? Mind-blowing if you actually know him.'

'Ah, Rude.' I shifted my position on the couch, and winced at my cuts.

'You cut yourself in all this?'

'I must have. I think when he landed on me with his shrinkens still in.'

'Shurikens,' Ellison corrected me.

'Anyway. I'm glad you both find it amusing that despite being so inept I managed to kill and behead a dude, but is there any chance that we could cut to the chase?' I looked at the mayor. 'Are you gunna turn us in?'

There was no mistaking it; he was aghast at the question. 'My dear boy! Not at all! In fact, I'll help you.'

'Why?'

'Because I just may need you.'

'What for?'

'I'll tell you in a bit. First, I want to know more about your harvesting job.'

'Well, I've only had one day...'

'Actually, go back a step. Why were you bad at vending? It's most unusual for a protégé to take up a trade other than what their master does.'

'I have dyscalculia.'

'Pardon?'

'I can't do maths.'

He looked at Ellison. 'And you gave up on him that quickly?'

'Not exactly, sir... the thing with Uly is, he's kind of... squeamish. And somewhat accident-prone.'

'Oh what? Don't tell people that!'

'He's squeamish about blood?' He was actually smirking.

'I'm not squeamish! I'm getting used to it and I'm not accident-prone, goddamn it! I'm just trying to acclimatise!'

They both regarded me silently, presumably because I used the word acclimatise.

'I can't help it if I'm a bit awkward! I'm trying my best! I've never even dissected a frog in science class! I can't help it if I don't wanna fuck around with dead bodies! It's creepy!'

The mayor held up a hand. 'Calm down, we're not attacking you, but I am confused about something, maybe you can help me understand.'

'Well, I'll try.'

'So, you don't really like to handle blood all that much, though I see you're becoming accustomed to ingesting it.'

'Yeah...'

'And the thought of killing humans is hard for you to take?'

'Well... yes it is. Only a few weeks ago, I was one. I know the rules. I know it all has to be random, but it doesn't make it any easier to like.'

'Yet, you burst in here like gangbusters and killed a vampire, just like that?'

'He was raping her! And he looked right at me! And licked his lips!'

'So you were doling out justice?'

'Yes! And I don't regret it! Even if I have to go to jail, or be put to death, or whatever!'

'Then why don't you do that for a job?'

'What?'

'Law enforcement.'

'You mean vampire government?'

'Precisely.'

'Well, I did think of that, but Ellison shot me down.' I looked at her. 'Sorry, but you did. It hurt.'

'Yeah, I did,' she shrugged, 'but that was before I knew you had any natural talent whatsoever. Telekinesis will only take you so far.'

The mayor cleared his throat. 'Squabbles aside, I think you may have found your calling, Ulysses. Being in my position has its perks. I have some strings I could pull. Would you be willing to try that?'

'Do I have to kill people?'

'Do you mean humans?'

'Yes.'

'Rarely. Government is more about enforcing vampire law within vampire communities. Keeping the eternal secret, maintaining the balance, that sort of thing.'

'Then yes, I would love to. If I never have to go into George's creepy basement again, it'll be too soon.'

'Then that's settled. Now, how about we clean up this mess?'

I couldn't help being reminded of Pulp Fiction. The mayor made some phone calls and after about half an hour, a small troop of guys arrived. None of them was Harvey Keitel though. I didn't shower, presuming I'd have to help, but they just wanted me out of the way. I wasn't about to get naked in front of all of them, so I just stood by the window and watched. Ellison joined me.

'What a day, huh?'

'You're telling me!'

'I never asked how your day was... with George...'

'Oh wow. So weird. Did you know he sits in the sun for an hour a day?'

She chuckled. 'No, but I'm not surprised. Did you help him kill anyone?'

'Are you serious?'

'Well, I asked him not to baby you.'

'You suck. But no, when I got there, the guy was already dead. He'd done it as we pulled up.' I shuddered.

'So you helped him drain the body?'

'Yeah... actually it was a bit interesting I guess... he showed me the ledger of all his orders. It's more in-depth than I'd thought it'd be.'

'What else did you do?'

'He showed me his death room, with all the tools and weapons. He took me shooting, too. Did you know he's got a little range?'

'I did, actually.'

'He made me shoot at a mannequin. I don't think he's right in the head.'

She chuckled again, softly. 'Did you kill the mannequin?'

'No. I missed every shot. It was a lady mannequin...'

'Yet you managed to sink that shuriken right in Dragomir's windpipe...'

'Yeah. Go figure...'

I turned around to look at the street. Ellison followed suit. 'We're gunna have to tell Manny.'

'Yes, you're right.'

'Does that mean he's free now?'

'Essentially, yes.'

'He might get himself into trouble with no guidance. He's a hot head.'

'That's what Government is for.'

We watched the cars endlessly pass for a while, in silence.

'Are you going to be ok?'

'I'll get over it.'

'I'm glad I killed him, you know.'

'I know.'

'I don't want anyone to treat you that way...'

'Ha! I bet you've thought of hate-fucking me a few times!'

'Yeah I guess... but that's cos you were treating me like shit. And, no matter what, I never would've raped you, even if I had the strength.'

'I know. I wouldn't have chosen you otherwise. You're a douche, not a monster.'

'Hm. So, where do we go from here?'

'Well, I guess we just continue with your training, and get you ready for your new career.'

'So is this Ruby thing really just going to go away?'

'Looks like it. Thankfully, you made a real mess of Dragomir. The mayor is impressed. He's always on the lookout for new Government; the turnover is somewhat high.'

'Why?'

'It's a hard job; not everyone is cut out for it I suppose.'

'What're we gunna do with Ruby's blood?'

'We're not going to do anything with it.' She turned around and discreetly pointed towards the door, where it had been sitting. It was no longer there.

'Where is it?' I whispered.

'Already gone, the mayor saw to that. He'll keep it for himself, probably. The point is, we don't have to sell it and I couldn't be happier.'

'Brilliant...' We stood there together until there wasn't any trace of Dragomir left. It was amazing, how they worked. They very clearly had done this before, many times. His remains were double bagged and put in moving boxes. On the outside of them they wrote things like 'books', and 'kitchen'. Out they took him on sack trucks. I looked out the window and watched them load him into a moving truck, no big deal. They scrubbed and scrubbed the floor, then scrubbed it again in the cracks with toothbrushes. They even cleaned my shurikens and the knife.

When the last one of them left, the mayor shut the door, but left his hand on the knob. He turned to us. 'This officially never happened. The poor lady you killed, Ulysses, Dragomir... you don't have to worry about any of it. Dragomir's protégé will need to be told, but we'll take care of it. He may approach you, and when he does, you know nothing. Am I making myself clear?'

'Yes, sir.' She nodded. He looked to me.

'Ulysses?'

'Oh. Yes, sir, definitely.'

'Good. Ulysses, I'll be in touch. Don't worry about harvesting. Keep practicing your mind control.' He opened the door.

'Sir?'

'Yes?'

'May I ask... why did you come here tonight?'

'Oh... I'm moving out of town, retiring. I just wanted to say thank you for providing such a wonderful service.'

'Oh, well thank you sir, it's been a pleasure working for you.'

'Oh you still will be. I'd like you to deliver to my new residence, if you don't mind?'

'Oh yeah, sure, no problem sir, I'd love to.'

'Great. I'll be in touch. Goodbye for now.'

Ellison shut the door behind him and leaned her forehead on it for a second, turned around and looked at me. 'Shower time; we're disgusting.'

'Ah sure. You wanna go first?'

She said nothing, just took me by the hand and led me there. I was nervous; I didn't know what she wanted and there was no way I was going to instigate anything sexual, especially given how this all started. We undressed and got under the water together. She turned me around and slowly washed my back. It felt so good and I had to really focus not to get a boner. She washed my hair. She spun me around again and cleaned every bit of blood off. She stopped, and I didn't realise I'd closed my eyes. I opened them, and she was holding the sponge out for me. I took it, and as carefully and non-sexually as possible, washed her. I hoped I was washing all the Dragomir off. Once I was done, she took the sponge off me, dropped it at our feet and lay her head on my chest. I wrapped my arms around her and we stood there, under the water until it started to run cool. I turned it off and draped a towel around her shoulders; she headed towards the bed and sat looking out the window. I dried myself and sat beside her. She lay her head on my shoulder.

'Just to clarify: tonight is definitely not a sex night, right?'

'That's right it isn't, but it can be a cuddle night, if you'd like that?'

'I would.'

We lay down. I put out my arm and she lay on it. I'd never done that before and was surprised to find it felt nice. Her skin was cool as she laid her cheek on my chest. She said nothing, and I was too scared to open my mouth and screw it up, so we just lay there. I thought about the past few weeks. I thought about the deaths I'd caused and the circus that had followed. I thought of that dead man today, and all those bags filling to be sold and consumed. I thought of Ellison's face when I opened that door. I started to wonder what bizarre thing might happen to me the next day when I realised I was falling asleep. I wondered how much longer I would need to sleep...